CW01510169

THE FAITHFULS

THE FAITHFULS

A 100% UNFAITHFUL PARODY
OF THE TRAITORS

HUW DUNNIT

WITH BRUNO VINCENT

abacus
books

*With sincere thanks to Hope M, and
Steve & Halina Dumughn!
This book is dedicated with fondness and
gratitude to Mike McGrath*

ABACUS

First published in 2025 by Abacus

1 3 5 7 9 10 8 6 4 2

A CIP catalogue record for this book is available from the British Library.

ISBN 978-0-349-14804-5

Typeset in Bembo by M Rules
Printed and bound in Great Britain by Clays Ltd, Elcograf S.p.A.

Papers used by Abacus are from well-managed forests
and other responsible sources.

Abacus
An imprint of
Little, Brown Book Group
Carmelite House
50 Victoria Embankment
London EC4Y 0DZ

The authorised representative
in the EEA is
Hachette Ireland
8 Castlecourt Centre
Dublin 15, D15 XTP3, Ireland
(email: info@hbgi.ie)

An Hachette UK Company
www.hachette.co.uk

www.littlebrown.co.uk

The scream echoed along the corridors, through the halls, up the stairwells, all the way through the castle.

'Oh, stop that,' said Manny Claudwinkle. 'Get a hold of yourself.'

'But he's dead,' she said. 'He's actually dead. He's actually really *dead!*'

'Darling, don't be so ridiculous,' Manny said, with half a smile. 'This isn't real life. This is television.'

As she spoke she stroked the other woman's arm to calm her. With her other hand she put two fingers to the man's neck. Felt around. Felt some more.

Then under her breath she said the rudest word she knew.

He was actually, really *dead.*

In the Castle

Crew

Manny Claudwinkle – glamorous presenter
Damian Shraw – anxious producer
Solaris Benedicta – diligent make-up artist
Hassan MacDougal – charming catering man
Yukio Nagataki – capable camera technician

Faithfuls

FlaymeZ, 23, Berkshire, physically enhanced beauty influencer
Keith, 53, Barking, road worker – bronzed, cheerful, straightforward
Fiona, 56, Glasgow, teacher with an expression of unamused granite
Elliott, 37, Hackney's 97th most in-demand grime DJ
Amina, 34, Sidcup, not entirely unmousy IT consultant
Harry, 60, Islington, artist, loud laugh, splendid clothes, head like an egg
Cecil, 66, Lincolnshire, portly and balding member of the political class
Louis, 25, Cornwall, shy and trembling giant of a motorbike mechanic
Enwyn, 53, Llangollen's most cheerful gardener
Judith, 45, Gloucester, mother-of-two, quiet and observant

Cops

Inspector Constable – lead investigator
PC Handcock – maker of tea

Chapter One

The detective came out onto the roof and held his hat. Turned away, swearing, for a moment. Then bent into the wind and stepped deliberately forward. In front of him was a helicopter with its blades spinning, and a man in a pilot's uniform looking disgustingly cheerful.

'You all good?' the pilot asked him.

'I hate murders, and I hate helicopters even more.'

The pilot gave him a thumbs up and hopped up into his seat. There was a spare space in the back for the young PC who was accompanying him on the journey.

As the craft lifted into the air the inspector closed his eyes. He did not open them as it banked into the wind and scudded across the city skyline.

'I like to call this route the Hollywood Walk of Fame,' said the pilot merrily, speaking through the earphones as the chopper left the city environs and crossed the countryside.

'Down there, that's the bridge they used for the train to Hogwarts in Harry Potter,' said the pilot. 'And that there is the castle they used in one of the Narnia films. Just over that hill *there* is where they filmed that car chase in the last James Bond. Yeah. Scenic as all buggery, this countryside.'

He looked over at the cop, who gave him a thumbs up.

'Got to admit, I bloody love it,' said the pilot. 'Best place in the world, when the weather's not horrible. So you like being a copper, eh?'

He looked at the policeman, who gave him another thumbs up.

'Ah, rather you than me. Grisly business. Solving murders? Tough stuff. I'd rather be in the sky, up here with the birds. Being a policeman's dangerous, they say. High incidence of alcoholism and suicide, I've heard. Is that right?'

The cop gave another cheerful thumbs up. Then saw from the other man's expression that this wasn't the expected response. And pulled one of the earpieces away from his head.

'I can't hear a bloody word you're saying, mate!' he bellowed.

The inspector looked down and saw they were descending towards their destination. The castle where they filmed that TV show, *The Faithfuls*. His wife and kids loved it. Look at all those scene-of-crime white tents. From above it looked like a bloody Christian music festival.

How many deaths were confirmed now? the detective wondered. God almighty. Horrible stuff. He clutched his tummy as the chopper set down with a bump, then jumped down as soon as he could, glad to be on terra firma.

The local police were waiting for him. A grey-haired fellow, looking strained.

'Glad to have you here,' said the local chief. 'Much too

much death for us to handle ourselves. We need the experts. You're Inspector ...'

'Constable,' said the inspector. 'Inspector Constable.'

'Ah,' said the other, looking amused. He turned to the PC. 'Then your surname must be Inspector?'

'Er, no, sir,' said the PC. 'It's Handcock.'

'I see,' said the chief. 'Well, come with me ...'

Interview Excerpt

Interviewee: Spike

Age: 32

Appearance: Spike has shoulder-length hair and wears glasses. He has a slightly wistful expression and a middle-distance stare.

Spike: It's amazing to be in the castle, so exciting. And the other players are all so great — I love them all. Well, I love everybody really. Or I try to. Everyone's got a good side, deep down. I truly believe that, I really do. Everyone.

[Listens to question from the off-camera interviewer.]

Spike: Piers Morgan? Well I think he's just a soul in torment who's searching for the right path and could still turn into a really nice bloke. Me, I'm a teacher. I teach primary school . . .

[Insert: A shot of Spike in his classroom, sat on a chair in front of five- and six-year-olds. He's playing the guitar and singing a hymn to them while they watch, and one kid picks their nose.]

Spike: It's so meaningful being a teacher. It can be hard work but it gives a great sense of fulfilment. I won't always be one though. You see, in truth, I've got another identity. [Looks into camera and speaks sincerely.] In fact, I believe that I am reincarnated from someone you might have heard of: Jesus Christ Our Lord. Or Yeshua, as he was really known. Me, as *I* was really known. I mean, how much more faithful can you get?

[Listens to another question off mic.]

Spike: [Nods thoughtfully.] Yes, as you say, I'm thirty-two now, so . . . [Shrugs.] next year's going to be a big one for me . . .

FATE ON *THE FAITHFULS*: KILLED BY THE MURDERERS — EPISODE 1

Chapter Two

B right sunshine flooded in through the windows.
For once, the whole family was sat round the
breakfast table.

'We're all here at the same time!' said Manny. 'How
often does that happen these days?'

In the middle of the table was a bowl of scrambled eggs,
a plate covered with toast, a much-gouged block of butter.

'Darling,' said her husband. He was looking at her dead
in the eyes.

Manny laughed. 'What's up with you?' she said.

'Darling, I love you with all my heart. The last twenty
years together have been the best of my life.'

Manny straightened her back. This was probably the
build-up to some sort of joke. She waited. He still hesitated, so she said, 'Go on ...'

'But these last few years, I hardly ever see you. I feel like
I don't know who I'm married to any more.'

Manny kept her expression still, but inside, her heart
flipped over. Not in front of the kids. We know why I'm
doing this! It's securing our future ...

'Mummy,' said Vee, her four-year-old.

Manny turned, bemused, to her. Put her hand out to hold Vee's hand. The little one was fixing her with a steady, intent expression too.

'I'll never stop loving you, Mummy,' said Vee. 'You're the best mummy I could have.'

'Glad to hear it . . .' Manny said. She didn't like all this seriousness. She flicked back her fringe.

'But you forgot my birthday,' said Vee. 'It made me very sad.'

'I didn't *forget*,' said Manny, getting hot under the collar. 'It was a work emergency. I told you how sorry I was . . . Daddy was here . . . I sent a present . . . and didn't I make it up to you with the trip to—'

'Mum,' said Milo, her teenager. He'd always been her biggest fan, admired her television career and forgiven her failings because he thought she was so brilliant. Now, to her horror, she saw coldness in his eyes, too.

'Hey, boy,' she said. 'What's up? What is this?'

'I really wanted you to see me in *Julius Caesar*. You helped me audition, and it was amazing when I got the part. But . . .'

'It really kills me to do this,' said her husband. 'But I have to vote for someone. And also, you promised never to wear that wig inside the house. And therefore I'm voting for: you, darling.'

He turned over the slice of toast he'd had in his hand, and it had *Darling* written on it in flowing script made from melting butter.

Manny stared at it. How did he write that, with his breakfast knife?

'I don't want to vote for anyone,' said Vee, solemnly,

sucking in her little cheeks and looking around the room for a moment before her eyes came to rest on her mother. 'But I have to. And so – I'm afraid it's you.'

She flipped over the piece of brown toast in her hands. On it was written in the same yellow text: *Mummy*.

Manny's temperature was quickly rising. This wasn't funny any more.

'Milo,' she said softly.

He blinked back tears as he turned over a slice of toast on which was written: *Mum*.

'*Et tu, Brute?*' she asked. And she wanted to tell the kids to eat their toast. To eat it up and get a good breakfast for goodness sake. The day ahead would have challenges, with betrayal and in-fighting, and wasn't breakfast the most important meal of the day? Have some eggs as well, they were going cold.

But she couldn't open her mouth to speak.

She *had* been away for Vee's birthday, she *had* missed the three performances of *Julius Caesar* at the East Dulwich Academy, and she *had* abandoned her marriage bed these past twelve weeks, and indeed for five months a year for the past seven years . . .

She wanted to open her mouth to protest. But nothing came out. She knew that all she could do was get up and walk out, never to return. She had been voted out.

Manny sat up in bed, her heart hammering. Terrified by the total darkness for a moment before she realised she was wearing her owl-eyes sleep mask and ripped it off.

Had she forgotten her daughter's birthday? She couldn't have!

She looked around. Where was she?

God, her heart wouldn't stop thumping.

Then she realised it wasn't her heart. It was the hotel room door.

'Ms Claudwinkle?' came a voice through it. 'This is your morning alarm call! The car is here for you!'

She looked at her alarm clock.

5.15.

Chapter Three

'You know why I've asked you all here . . .' she said. 'The prize pot stands at seventy-seven thousand pounds. And now it's decision time.'

All the castle's guests were gathered in the Mead Hall. Sat around the Dodecahedral Table, glancing nervously at each other.

'This is the heart of *The Faithfuls*. The moment of truth. It's time to vote out who you think is the Murderer . . .'

Manny stalked slowly around the perimeter of the room, looking them all in the eye, one by one. They quaked solemnly, like jurors at a murder trial.

'I hope you get it right,' she said, with insinuating menace. 'Because if you don't, you'll be doing the Murderer's work for them.'

The guests looked at each other. Friends and allies exchanged glances. Others stared mistrustfully from beneath furrowed brows.

'We know that there is at least one Murderer in this room,' she said. 'But is there more than one?'

The setting of the sumptuous Mead Hall, the

flickering light on the tapestry on the wall, intensified the atmosphere.

The contestants were fighting for their lives. Fighting to stay in the game, and on TV screens around the world.

Me too, darling, thought Manny.

Making TV, staying in the spotlight, was always a cut-throat business. It never got easy. And just when everyone thought you were on top of the world was exactly when things could be most difficult.

Here she was, presenting the most popular programme on television. In its seventh glorious year at the top of the ratings.

But behind the scenes, the production company was cutting costs. Well, that wasn't exactly true. The production company's parent company's *parent* company, based in Zurich, were.

And, strange to say, television production was not their forte. It made up a comparatively small part of an enormous pie. Overall, the conglomerate owned more than seventy companies, manufacturing luxury cars, toys, industrial solvent, curtain rods, aeronautical parts, colour dye and hundreds of other items.

TV production was for them a small, mildly interesting sideline. There were always costs that could be cut.

The ratings of *The Faithfuls* had maintained their Himalayan altitudes through seasons five and six, and despite a stated desire by the bosses that the show end on a high rather than fizzling out, they had reluctantly greenlit a seventh season.

With a skeleton crew. Even 'skeleton crew' was generous. This was a skeleton on Ozempic. One make-up person, fixed cameras operated remotely by one cameraman, a single lad in a catering van making food and drinks for everyone.

The contestants had no idea – they were so excited to be here, they couldn't know how it was changed from previous seasons. *Series*, she told herself. When did we Brits start saying 'seasons'?

'I'm going to speak first if I may,' said a young woman, adjusting her bright blonde hair. She pouted. 'Keith,' she said, turning to a larger middle-aged man a few seats away. 'I'd like to ask you something.'

Keith, a road worker, smiled at her placidly. 'Darling,' he said.

'You know I love you,' she said. He nodded. 'I'm just wondering what you meant this morning when you said that Fiona had some questions to answer. I thought you and Fiona was good mates.'

Keith nodded again. 'I wanted to play a board game with her,' he said. 'That's all. Me and Fiona are great mates aren't we, Fiona?'

A stony-faced woman with short gunmetal-coloured hair on the other side of the table agreed with him. But looked thoughtful as she did it.

'I just thought it was a funny way to say it,' said the young woman.

'Exactly,' said Keith. 'Just a joke – a silly way of saying, I was looking for her to play *Trivial Pursuit*.'

'A joke,' said the young woman. 'But I was wondering, was there maybe some truth in it? You were trying to open up a conversation maybe.'

Keith was still smiling, but looking a tad frustrated. 'Nope – just a joke, nothing more.'

'There's a little bit of truth in every joke,' said a man sitting next to Keith.

Keith had to turn his whole body round to look at him.

'Is there, Elliott?' he said. 'I mean – why did the hedgehog cross the road? To see his flatmate. There's no truth in that.'

The room thought about this for a moment.

'It contains a truth of violence towards hedgehogs,' said Elliott. 'Which is a problem in our society.'

'I personally love hedgehogs,' said the young woman, touching her heart ever so gently with her painted finger-nails, which were an inch longer than her fingers. 'They're *beautiful*. And I think we could find that a bit distasteful.'

'It seems to me to show an underlying concern with death,' said Elliott. 'Even murder, maybe.'

Keith opened his mouth, his expression caught between a laugh and an expostulation of defence.

'Subconsciously, I mean,' said Elliott. 'You don't even know you're showing that side to us.'

'All I wanted was a game of bloody *Trivial Pursuit*,' Keith muttered. 'I couldn't even find the damn game, someone had moved the box . . .'

'And now you're being defensive,' said the young woman, pityingly. 'Which tells its own story.'

'Okay, you've had enough time,' Manny said, still walking slowly around the table, her heels clicking against the stone flags.

'But I wanted to ask Harry about—' Keith said.

'Sorry, Keith,' Manny replied. 'That is time. You must all now vote . . .'

Glances were exchanged across the table, some smug and knowing, some sceptical and doubtful, as people wrote down the name of their chosen victim. Keith looked decidedly uncomfortable.

One by one, they were invited to turn over their cards.

'I'm sorry, Keith,' said one.

'It kills me to do this, Keith,' said another.

'Something just doesn't add up, Keith,' said a third.

Keith struggled manfully with the injustice of it. And accepted every fresh betrayal with a stiff nod, or a sad smile.

'Keith,' Manny said. 'I'm afraid you have to leave the castle for ever. Now, please tell us . . .'

Keith came to stand in front of the crackling fire, facing the table and their judgement. Above him on the stone wall were two crossed medieval weapons, a pike and a battle-axe.

'I've had the time of my life on this show,' he said. 'And I can now reveal that I was, all along . . . *one of the Faithfuls.*'

Gasps of horror and shock rippled through the room as he strode out.

'And cut,' said Manny, relaying the instruction she'd received through the earpiece that was hidden beneath her wig.

Interview Excerpt

Name: Jeannie
Age: 67
Appearance: Kind, gentle face with wrinkles
of good humour around the mouth and eyes,
Jeannie is in a purple cardigan with a
flowery silk scarf tied around her neck.

Jeannie: Oh, yes, I'd *love* to be one of
the Secret Murderers. Who would suspect a
kind, little old lollypop lady of being a
Murderer? But just because I spend all day
protecting the sweet children's lives, and
making the roads safe, doesn't mean that
I'm not allowed to do a bit of murdering of
adults in my spare time! [Giggles naughtily.]

[Cut to later in the interview.]

Jeannie: I think I'm in with a good chance. I like to say I'm a real *Jeannie in a bottle*, ha ha! I'm friendly, I love to make friends. You know what, I want to get to know some younger people properly. Get to understand their lives. This Al person they're all worried about, for instance. Who seems to threaten their jobs. Who is he? I'm so keen to know! You see his name everywhere, Al this, Al that, Al the other. Al *who*, I want to know?

[Listens to a remark from the interviewer.]

Jeannie: *A.I.*? [Visibly mystified.] Well, okay, he's called A.I., then. But what's his *surname*?

FATE ON *THE FAITHFULS*: VOTED OFF — EPISODE THREE

Chapter Four

Cameras on the walls discreetly watched as the con-testants surged out of the Mead Hall, along an oak-panelled passageway and into the socialising rooms: an oak-panelled drawing room, an oak-panelled games room and a modern kitchen area filled with modern conveniences (but, behind these, the kitchen was also panelled with oak).

There, they hugged and wept, soul-searched, wondered what they could be doing wrong – to have voluntarily sacrificed yet another of the Faithfuls. Quietly, too, they compared theories and plotted in their twos and threes. Who could they trust?

They needed time to be together without the production crew, and also this footage was gold, so Manny marched to the front door where the director-producer was waiting for her.

Last year they'd had a separate director and producer, and an assistant director to boot, and the producer had had a team of six bustling around offering coffees, prepping the next shot, managing the flower budget. Now it was just the two of them.

It didn't matter, she told herself. Nothing mattered. Just

make the show, and make it brilliant. The more obstacles you put in my way the more determined I am.

The producer-director, Damian Shraw, was short, fifty-five, obsessively clean and utterly stressed.

He walked her over the gravel drive towards the catering truck, taking out his hand sanitiser and nervously decontaminating himself, despite the fact that he hadn't touched anything.

'Got three things for you,' he said without preamble. 'Did you read—'

'Poor Keith,' Manny said. 'Stitched up like a kipper. Have you got any kippers today, Hassan?'

'Nah I ain't got no kippers, love,' said the catering man. 'Not today. Do you a flat white though?'

'You're an angel,' Manny said.

'You've really got to read your production messages, Manny,' said Damian. 'There's a lot of important little things we don't have time to discuss. Look, I've actually printed them off for you.' He handed her a manila folder which she tucked under one arm. 'Now, there's something wrong with the car fleet today. I'm trying to fix it.'

'Wrong how?' Manny said. '*All* of them?'

'The firm won't drive today. They say there's going to be a storm. It won't be safe to get up here.'

'I'm just going to do your cheeks, love,' said the make-up woman, or Head of Beauty (a job title she'd selected for herself). Ordinarily, Manny would ask to be left alone while having a conference with her fellow producer, but she got the sense from Damian's demeanour that she was about to be told off, and so didn't mind someone else being here to mitigate his irritation.

Also, she liked being made up. She spent a lot of every day being made up, by herself or others. It was when she did her thinking. It practically made her purr. And even more, she liked saying the make-up woman's name to herself: Solaris Benedicta. It was so beautiful. She liked rolling it around on her tongue. Solaris Benedicta . . .

Manny looked around. It was overcast, with just the slightest breeze.

'Doesn't look like a storm,' she said. 'It's pretty bloody warm for Scotland, I'd say.'

'Apparently the cows are sitting down,' said Damian, looking vexed.

'The *taxi* drivers won't drive because the cows are *sitting down*?' Manny asked.

'Just stay still, love,' said Solaris. 'I'll have to do that bit again.'

'What are they, farmers?' Manny asked.

'Well, yes,' said Damian. 'They were farmers until five years ago when we bought their land so we could play all these outdoor games on it. They got themselves cars to ferry us to the mainland. When the cows sit down, there's going to be a big one.'

'What does the weather service say?' Manny asked.

'Just try and stay still, love,' said Solaris.

'Flat white, oat, no caff, sweetener,' said Hassan.

'You're an angel, an *archangel*,' said Manny. 'A god!'

'The weather up here changes on a sixpence,' said Damian. 'But the upshot is, I'm driving Keith back now. I'll find another taxi firm in town and come back later to fetch you all. But it's . . .'

'Not ideal,' said Manny.

'No,' said Damian. 'For insurance purposes I've got to be on site at all times. Just make sure everyone's safe and stays indoors.'

'Of course, you've got it,' said Manny.

Used to intense sixteen-hour-a-day shoots as she was, sitting around and doing nothing for a few hours was something she could handle.

She turned back to the house and felt suddenly buffeted by wind. Her coffee sploshed a few drops which she managed not to get on herself. There was the bang of a window shutter. She looked up at the castle. Was it her imagination or was it somehow larger and uglier than it had been before? It seemed to loom more against the suddenly moody sky.

Chapter Five

E veryone has secrets.

The contestants had several hours to gather, to talk. To make friends, to suss out enemies. They were mic'd up at all times during the day. While they shared secrets, and tried to winkle out each other's, their own were being rigorously recorded.

There was one place on the whole castle estate that was the locus of the greatest secrecy, the direst fear, the most hideous betrayal. This was the Secret Murderers' Lodge, a location by now almost as recognisable in TV-land from its iconography as the TARDIS.

It was carefully filmed from above to appear like the highest turret in a tottering gothic castle. This was where the Murderers gathered in sepulchral gloom, enrobed like a cluster of mad monks to plan which of the Faithfuls they would mercilessly execute.

(The viewers were encouraged – by a video insert of the Secret Murderers wandering around the grounds in the dead of night in cloaks, holding flaming torches and look-ing like they were on their way to a late-night orgy with

Anne Boleyn – to believe these meetings were at midnight. In fact they were at six p.m. sharp, before the taxi back to the hotel for a sauna and dinner.)

In fact it was an anonymous – and from the outside thoroughly basic – gardener's shed with a rusty corrugated iron roof and a fire barrel in the centre. It stank not of elixirs and burning wax, as viewers might expect, but petrol, decaying cigarette stubs and wet straw.

Bathetically, into this locus of horror and perfidy (but away from where the cameras pointed) had been crammed a little settee, a table with a mini fridge under it and a kettle so that Manny could retreat there when she needed, or when she was not needed by others.

She hunted around for one of those bland protein bars she was allowed by her dietician to eat. She felt sure there must be one somewhere, and scrabbled down the side of the little sofa. She looked irritably under the pillows.

Hers was a very strict diet. Her silhouette was, for a woman of her age (albeit the precise age was never disclosed to the public), quite extraordinary. She still had a thigh gap – a visible diamond of space at the top of her legs, when filmed straight on.

The thigh gap (or rather filming it, displaying it to the public) was actually considered irresponsible among girls and younger women – an actress or celebrity in their twenties or thirties with such a gap was thought to be a bad role model, to be setting unrealistic body standards to young women which could have bad mental-health outcomes for viewers. It was (or could be) frowned upon. (In fact, one must try to remember that these days, everything that *could* be frowned upon, *was*. One should no longer use the conditional tense when talking about public disapproval.)

In someone who was born during the government of Ted Heath, however, the possession of a thigh gap was widely seen as a cause of admiration, astonishment and awe.

Anyhonk.

She sat heavily on the sofa. Where could that nut bar be? There had to be one somewhere around the place . . . She felt exhausted, and the day was only half done. Manny sincerely felt the pressure and the emotion of the players. She felt they were hers, and it was her job to look after them, their hopes and fears. She loved them. She experienced the feelings that they felt.

It was her absolute determination to make this cold, brutal game about betrayal and murder into a warm-hearted, emotional experience.

In order for this season – series – to go ahead, she'd had to become a producer. It was required that there be two producers. And there was no budget for two producers. So she had taken on the role, and offered to be paid a reduced salary to keep the show on the road.

There were extra tasks involved, but she was being slow in incorporating them into her working day. She had only so much energy. Supervising murder was taxing.

Working in TV was undoubtedly glamorous from the outside. But from within, there was a ridiculous sequence of compromises to deal with. For instance, here she was presenting the biggest show in the UK, and doing it practically on her own.

Any viewer would surely think this was madness. But the way it worked, the money for every new series had to be found from scratch. You didn't get your budget from the leftover profits from previous series, like it was in some sort of slush fund. Those monies had all disappeared into shareholders' pockets. You had to argue for every damn penny.

And because you were appealing to a company with so many tendrils and tentacles, you might suddenly experience restricted cashflow because a dry summer meant a depleted haricot-bean crop in Uruguay, or a union bust-up in Mongolia caused an aluminium shortage that made tennis-racquets forty per cent more expensive, affecting the profitability of the whole group.

The Faithfuls had been sold all over the world. It was a stunningly profitable piece of intellectual real estate – with home-grown versions already broadcast in thirty-two countries, and regular audiences in the region of half a billion people.

But there were more millions and billions to be made. The television industry had long been looking for the next big thing. And naturally Manny was positioned to be in on that next big thing, and wanted to be.

You've got to read the proposals though. You've got to read your pages. And most of the time when she wasn't 'on' (i.e. on camera, or waiting for the camera to roll), her brain was zonked. She'd even resorted to paying her children to read out TV proposals while she lay on the sofa with a moist towelette on her forehead. Which probably wasn't giving them (the proposals that is) a fair shot, but after a long day of filming *I Insist You Accompany Me Dancing*, it was the best she could do.

Please, promise me, you'll read your reports, Damian had said. *It's important.*

Manny picked up the folder and opened it. Practically an inch-thick wad of paper within. Goddamn it, Damian must have printed out practically every email she'd ever received. How did he know that she wasn't reading them? And also – hello? The planet? Was 'Please consider the environment before printing this email' invisible to him? (Actually she noticed that this wasn't actually on the bottom of emails any more, for some reason.)

She tutted.

And started to read.

She instantly felt her head swoon slightly. She just couldn't take it in. She sighed and let the pages flop onto her chest.

I've probably got ADHD or one of those modern diseases young people have, she thought, feeling exhausted.

Poor Keith. Poor next person too. Lambs to the slaughter! At the thought of lamb, she felt her tummy rumble and looked around for the flavourless nut bar.

God, I love television, Manny thought as she checked under the sofa. *God, I'm tired.*

It was no good, the bar had been snaffled by fate, or time, or a mouse, or Yukio the cameraman. She was just going to make herself sneeze sniffing all this floor dust, and mess with her make-up. She *must* read those pages. She picked them up again and flopped back onto the sofa.

She realised with a start that Damian must be disappointed with her, if he'd bothered to print off her notes. There were important things in there. Possibly something that he didn't want or was afraid to say to her out loud. Something she ought to keep her eye on.

Interview Excerpt

Interviewee: Jeremy

Age: 35

Appearance: Back-combed wavy black hair, tanned and comfortable looking in a Jermyn Street shirt. When he itches his nose we see he sports a signet ring.

Jeremy: I'm just a completely ordinary person, I think. I'm a solicitor who does conveyancing. I do a spot of gardening and I like Formula One. Happily married to my wonderful wife. It's a quiet life. So yeah: just an ordinary guy.

Being boring is my plan, you see — I'm a big fan of the show. I've watched every series. The international versions too. And I've got a theory. The way to get through

to the later rounds is to be quiet and
unnoticeable. But just to be *double* sure, I
want to get people's sympathy. So I'm going
to pretend I've got severe brain damage and
can't talk properly. Clever, right? It was
my wife's idea. I do love her, she's just so
much more intelligent than I am.

**FATE ON *THE FAITHFULS*: VOTED OFF —
EPISODE ONE**

**(Went into hiding with family after online
campaign.)**

Chapter Six

'I 'll be back as soon as I can,' said Damian, looking in through the door of the Secret Murderers' Lodge.

Manny did not like being startled, especially startled awake, most especially startled awake by her boss with drool running down her chin, and a sheaf of papers she was supposed to be reading splayed guiltily over her chest.

'Where's my nut bar?' she demanded. 'There was one here. You stole it!'

She scrambled to her feet, grabbed her papers and followed him out, talking about aspects of the production and asking a few more questions while he got into his car.

'Good luck,' said Damian, applying hand sanitiser and rubbing his mitts vigorously before allowing himself to touch his own steering wheel. 'I'll be ninety minutes. Two hours max.'

'Bye,' she said. 'And bye, Keith! You didn't steal my nut bar, did you?' He shook his head innocently.

'Wouldn't touch that muck,' he said, his voice barely audible through the glass.

And Damian drove off, away from the estate and onto the Sea Road.

So the contestants are stuck with just me for the time being, Manny thought. *I'll be all right. Everything will be fine.*

Bloody hell, I hope nobody throws up or gets a nosebleed or something.

No, she told herself. *I'll be fine. We'll all be!*

I already take care of them, after all. I feel I look after them. I'll just have to look after them for the next hour or two, that's all. The thought made her sit up for a moment, like she'd had a little electric shock.

She remembered the first time she'd come to scout this location, by helicopter, on a clear May day eight years earlier. The bold castle standing on its little rise, encircled by a pretty moat, with woods all around, and the lakes. How stunning it had seemed.

And then just a couple of miles away, the rearing, roaring ocean.

'My god, this place is exposed!' she'd said.

'It's the edge of the world. That's what makes it perfect,' the producer (now long gone – working on a Netflix cheerleader documentary) told her merrily. 'It's private, no one can bother us, we have all this land to ourselves.'

Manny had jabbed a finger at the frighteningly narrow spit of land connecting the place they were looking at with the mainland.

It was hard to be heard over the sound of the helicopter, and so she just jutted her finger all the harder. And raised her eyebrows.

'Perfect,' said the producer, again. 'When the show's a hit, it will mean there's no prying eyes from paparazzi trying to guess who's got through to what round. Total privacy.'

'Not dangerous, then?' asked the decidedly city-reared Manny, a woman who liked her comforts.

The producer just smiled at her. It was one of the frustrating lessons she'd learnt in life, as it went on: people just smile and pretend to listen, and that's how they make things your problem. A speck of darkness sped fast across the landscape far beneath – the helicopter's shadow.

'It really is beautiful,' said Manny. From up here, she felt she could see the curve of the horizon. 'You know, we really *could* make a tremendous TV series here . . .'

The producer had just smiled.

But then, in a helicopter dazzled by light reflected from the ocean, and with total confidence that they were about to make a brilliant series, it was easy to be won over, and to forget the first, major thought that had crowded into her mind: *God, what a lonely and dangerous place!*

A slender promontory, leading to a lump of rock sticking out into the ocean.

What if anything went wrong?

'My idea is that we will make it appear as though we're in the middle of the Scottish Highlands,' the producer said, 'rather than on a little island. Film lots of the games elsewhere. Make it look not so – so wee, and fragile.'

Manny nodded, looking down. *If something went seriously wrong here, what would you do, where would you go?* It's just a castle – a big house really – all on its own.

Everything is a risk. Everything is terrifying.

Her heart fluttered.

For someone who as a girl was terrified to get out of

bed and go to school, sitting strapped into a helicopter is nothing. You endure one, you endure the other.

She'd felt the strap running over her lap and squeezed it lovingly. *Keep me safe, darling, there's a good girl*, she thought.

Now that was her. She was the seatbelt. Last line of defence.

And now the gravel on the drive scattered as Damian's car drove away. Keith glanced out of the back window, putting a brave face on it. She gave him a sincere smile and waved.

Interview Excerpt

Interviewee: Rick
Age: 26
Appearance: Rick is a relaxed lad in baggy
blue jeans and a fashionable black parka
done up to the neck.

Rick: I'm easy-going, I like to get on with
people. I think I'll have a good time in the
castle. I like everyone I've met so far. A
really good bunch . . .

[Cut to later in the conversation.]

Rick: I'm currently unemployed, so the prize
money will mean a lot to me, of course. My
poor mum often doesn't see me for months or
years at a time, so I'd like to help her out
with a few quid. You know what I mean?

[Listens to a question.]

Rick: Do I have any secrets? Interesting question. Well ... Rick isn't actually my real name, as it happens! Actually it's someone else's identity. I sort of ... borrowed it. It, um, 'wasn't convenient to be me' at that point. Actually I borrowed that explanation off someone too. I admit it. These glasses? Are they yours, mate? Oh, sorry. No, I just found them.

[Takes sunglasses off and hands them back to someone off screen. There's a further remark from off screen. A hand comes in front of the camera, pointing to a bulge in Rick's parka.]

Rick: What's that, mate? Er, dunno what you mean.

[He is reluctantly obliged to unzip his top and inside a golden candlestick is revealed.]

Rick: Oh yeah right. I forgot that was in there. I was just borrowing it.

FATE ON *THE FAITHFULS*: ONE OF THE SECRET MURDERERS, SUCCESSFULLY VOTED OFF — EPISODE FOUR

Chapter Seven

B eing murdered could be difficult.

Well, that's not exactly right.

It wasn't hard at all. In fact, in this castle it was bloody inevitable. But it was hard to do it *with class*.

There were two types of exit interviews: interviews for people who'd been voted off (such as the one Keith would be giving), and slightly more sinister affairs, where guests were informed they had been victims of the Secret Murderers. In these latter ones, they entered the interview room to find their status announced by a medieval scroll sealed with wax, sitting pertly on a chair.

The producers had decided that there would never be any bitterness on screen. Therefore every contestant was given a sufficient cooling-down period after being ejected from the show, before their final words were recorded. 'Keep it classy,' they were always encouraged.

Keith would have time for a bath and a lie down and maybe a pint of beer (or three) if he liked. In some cases a contestant sat down all calm composure until the cameras were running, when there was an explosion of tears or violent language. Occasionally it took a day or two, or when impossible they tried again a week or a month later, calling the contestant back out of the cold, into the studio. Sometimes it wasn't possible at all, and they gave up.

Manny turned to go back to the Secret Murderers' Lodge, but even though she knew she ought to try and have a lie down, she could feel already that she wasn't going to be able to get to sleep.

She always felt woozy and dissatisfied without anything specific to get on with. There was no scheduled task between now and a late lunch (although she could always launch another assault on the wad of unread documents), with the contestants being encouraged to spend a lot of time in each other's company, so that they would end up gossiping, forming friendship networks, suspecting and supporting each other. Same old, same old.

She looked at the folder of paper. Oh, sod that. She decided to walk around the castle instead. Maybe get a touch up of make-up or a full going over from scratch, after her cobwebby nut-bar search.

As she turned one corner of the castle, contemplating that Cobwebby Nut-bar Search might be the band name her son and his friends had been looking for, she was nearly swept off her feet.

'My god!' she said, and she didn't even hear the words coming out of her own mouth.

The wind was so strong it knocked the breath out of her.

Window shutters were banging hard against the castle wall, somewhere out of sight. It was not a relaxing sound and made one feel the taxi drivers-cum-farmers might be right about this 'storm' business.

Someone ought to stop that banging. Where's a bloody runner when you need one?

It's a sound person's nightmare, a real nuisance to the sound quality. But then the high wind was too. Probably anything that got recorded would need to be re-recorded, or be voiced over for it to be good enough quality to use.

Manny had worked at the top of television, on live Saturday-night shows in front of audiences of a thousand. All of a sudden she looked around and realised she couldn't think where the nearest production employee was.

She hesitated. They only had one runner on this series but he was a useless posh boy who had called in sick this morning anyway.

But that's mad, she thought. *There must be* . . . One by one, she ticked off the people who ought to be around. And the reasons why they weren't.

She walked round to the front of the castle to share this with Hassan. He was always good to chat to, always cheerful and funny. For a moment she thought she'd gone the wrong way and ended up at the far side of the schloss. This must be the rear of the castle . . .

But no. Here was the drawbridge. There were no exterior shots today so the staff were able to park outside the front for their own convenience, instead of in a clearing in the woods a quarter of a mile down the road.

Disappointment: the Head of Beauty's pink polka-dot Mini was gone. No more Solaris. That didn't seem right. And – could this be correct – the catering truck was gone! What if someone wanted something? No more Soleros! That was a crime!

Manny spun round and looked bemusedly at the frontage

37

of the castle. Her eyes scanned left and right as she thought, *No one to gossip with. No one to complain to.*

. . . except me. I'm in charge, I'm in loco parentis. *I really am* the seatbelt!

The thought gave her a slight twinge.

Nothing had better bloody go wrong, she thought.

Then she heard a scream.

Chapter Eight

The local police chief, Millard, was a rotund fellow, his tummy pressing out his smart uniform, all cleaned and buttons shining. He seemed to be puffed up, possibly by his elevation in the force, but (the inspector thought, looking at him critically) it might just as well have been by the device used to inflate tractor tyres. He had a few final flecks of red in his silver hair that were being tossed around in the wind from the helicopter rotor blades.

He walked Inspector Constable towards the first of the white scene-of-crime tents, which were billowing and straining in the wind, just like his hair.

'I'll be off, chief,' said the pilot in Constable's ear. 'I need to clear space for the next landing.'

'Yes, sure, bye,' said Constable over his shoulder, perplexed by the pilot's chattiness. Maybe it was lonely being on your own in a helicopter all the time. When he glanced to watch the fellow fly away, he saw another set of rotors in the sky up above, hovering and waiting to land.

'We've had to call experts in from all over Scotland,' said

Millard. 'In order to get to grips with this situation quickly. We've not had something so serious for decades, luckily. We've had to pull spare scene-of-crime officers from all the major cities.'

'Do we know if we still have a perpetrator at large?' Constable asked. 'That's the most important question right away.'

Millard gave him a heavy look.

'As I say. It's complex. I wish I could give you a definitive answer. But come with me . . .'

There was a white tent by the front door of the castle. Another by the entrance of a large barn-like outhouse fifty feet away and a third beside some crushed masonry nearly overhanging the edge of the moat.

There was a yet another tent just inside the large door, in the centre of the atrium. Atrium made it sound like an office block. Entrance hall?

Just yards inside, to the left, in a nearby games room, was a *fifth* tent. Constable whistled in disbelief. Unexpectedly, he received a wave in response from one of the officers who was bending down to brush particles from the carpet.

'The real action's out back, in the Mead Hall . . .' said Millard.

'Do we have a preliminary idea of what order things happened in?' he asked.

'I thought you ought to speak to the main witness,' said Millard. 'You realise that she's famous?'

'I'm told she is. But I don't know her myself.'

'Oh, I love her on *I Insist You Accompany Me Dancing*. I haven't spoken to her yet. Rather than just repeat ourselves, I thought I'd keep her fresh for you.'

'That's probably sensible . . .' said Constable, who then caught his breath coming through the door into the Mead Hall. 'Great mother of Christ,' he said.

It was white-tent city in here.

Chapter Nine

M anny looked around. Amina, one of the contestants, came out of the front door of the castle. She had her hand over her mouth.

'I know, darling,' said Manny. 'Catering van's gone – must have some sort of technical issue. I bet he'll be back before you know it. But for now – no flat whites. No Soleros!'

Amina stood still and stared at her.

'But we'll just have to grit our teeth and bear it,' Manny said. 'In fact, our teeth may be grateful for it. If it's a flat white you're after, there might be a sip of mine left . . .'

She held her cup out, shaking it to assure herself that it did indeed contain a final mouthful or so.

She assumed Amina had just been told she was suspected of being one of the Secret Murderers. It hit some people very hard when they were told they were suspected. In fact the show had to edit around their reactions very sensitively, with many a tearful session cut out.

There was something peculiar about this castle, or this TV-show format, which made people form amazingly intense relationships with each other – or claim to – very quickly. Feelings were intense and it made for a rollercoaster.

Best just to joke with her, be nice and cheerful, and try to snap her out of it.

She couldn't possibly have received any bad news from home, or have had any personal setbacks, as the cast were deliberately totally cut off from the outside world. Their phones were put in a black sack by Damian at the beginning of the day and placed in some secret location.

Which, Manny now realised, she did not know. (Probably the boot of his car, under a crate of hand sanitiser.)

She experienced another fleeting twinge of doubt at her ignorance. No doubt all this information that she didn't have was contained within the bunch of papers Damian had handed her, and which she was increasingly growing to resent and fear. She had another look at it. No way. Too thick. No one could read all that stuff.

So, logically, there was nothing that could have happened that could have genuinely deserved the response Amina was giving right now. She was overreacting.

I mean . . .

Unless something actually genuinely awful *had* happened, of course.

'Darling,' said Manny, holding the cup even higher. 'Sip of second-hand coff? It's the best I can do in the circs.'

She was not expecting Amina to take her up on it, but the contestant seemed to refocus her eyes, notice the cup. Then she took it and swallowed.

She handed the cup back.

'There's a dead body,' she said.

'Of course there is, darling,' said Manny. 'We're playing a game of murder here. There are bodies piled up around us left and right. Practically a Soviet purge.'

The wind billowing seemed to sober Amina up. She shook her head calmly.

'No, a real one,' she said.

'There can't be, that's ridiculous,' said Manny, already starting to feel that she was not reacting in the appropriate way.

'Well there is, Manny,' said Amina.

'Well there *can't be*,' said Manny.

Amina just stared at her.

Manny realised they were at an impasse. Normally someone else would have broken in by now. Yelled cut, or something. Why hadn't they?

I have absolutely no idea what to do, was the unspoken reply.

Interview Excerpt

Interviewee: FlaymeZ

Age: 23

Appearance: Long peroxided hair, false eyelashes, fake nails, enhanced lips

FlaymeZ: [Speaking in a decidedly posh drawl.] Well, of course, one doesn't like to boast about one's credentials. People might get the wrong idea if they know you were Head Girl at Chelly, better known as Cheltenham Ladies' College, and graduated in Philosophy (first-class honours) from Oxford. So, I altered my accent just a tiny little smidge-ette, to appear on the show. One likes to rub along with the common people, doesn't one, after all? That's what Berkshire used to say.

[Listens to question.]

FlaymeZ: Sorry — Grandaddy. I call him
Berkshire because he's the Earl of it. Used
to be great pals with Prince Philip. (My
godfather — lovely birthday pressies but
godawful halitosis.) They were partners at
real tennis. Berkshire thought Philly was
practically a hand-wringing liberal. Poor
Grandaddy, taken from us at just ninety-
five. Hang-gliding accident . . . [Wipes tear
from eye.]

Chapter Ten

C ome on brain, Manny thought. *Come on come on. What to do? Go and look, I suppose?* The thought made her feel sick.

Then she thought, *But wait. One way to stop there being a dead body would be if they hadn't died! Perhaps they might be resuscitated – it happens all the time!*

The thought galvanised her and she started marching inside.

'Tell me where it is, Amina,' she said.

But Amina didn't even have time to reply. The body took no finding. There it was, just inside the front door, sprawled in the middle of the entrance hall.

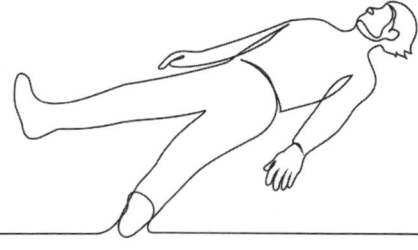

'My god,' said Manny. Up until now her panicking mind had concluded that either something really serious was going on, or Amina had gone insane. Which, after all, did in itself qualify as something really serious going on.

Either option had grave implications for the future of *The Faithfuls*.

Oh fuck. I've only been a producer on my own for less than quarter of an hour and it's all gone tits up already, she thought. After all, it was far too late to recast Amina, or anyone else. You couldn't just get to episode seven (which was roughly where they'd reached on this seaso— *series*) and then have a screen card which said: 'Sadly Amina went utterly doolally at this point and had to be removed from the show and popped in a white taxi to the funny farm.'

She was momentarily and self-deceptively relieved when she saw that the crumpled figure did not belong to anyone in the on-screen cast. She had also just had another thought: *There is one other grown-up on set who I can consult: Yukio, the cameraman. The all-knowing Yukio. Firm as a rock, trustworthy, unflappable. I'll ask him.*

Unfortunately that wasn't going to be possible. Yukio was certainly unflappable at the moment, but that was because it's very difficult to flap someone who's face down with a broken neck on a marble hallway floor.

Broken neck? Manny tilted her own neck to look from another angle.

It certainly didn't look like a very *well* neck. By no means a chiropractor's dream.

There were footsteps and another scream. Quieter, more muted, more abruptly halted.

In front of her was standing the contestant called Harry, in one of his stunning jackets, sliced into (or fabricated from) squares of yellow and purple and gold. Harry was sixty or so, with a shaved head and large, blocky glasses. You could tell at a glance that he was an artist – he could not be anything else. He had his hand over his mouth.

There now came footsteps from further away. Along passageways and down stairs from above. Some people arrived at the turn of the staircase and huddled there.

Manny looked around somewhat desperately. One ought to cover the body. Where did people in castles keep sheets? She supposed in some sort of closet like the rest of us . . .

She eyed a nearby velvet curtain, and although she rather fancied yanking it from the wall with a magnificent flourish, it was connected to a heavy gold curtain pole. Beneath one end of which was a large glass case containing a rather remarkably taxidermied family of ferrets. Frolicking in a rectangular glade of desiccated logs and dried grass.

All in all, what looked like six grand's worth of dead ferret. She was not knocking a hole in the budget that large just to cover a body.

'Oh god!' said someone coming down the stairs.

Here was one of the many little cliques who were scattered around the castle at any one time: Cecil, a portly late-middle-aged businessman, and next to him a large hulking lad of around twenty-five. This was Louis, a motorbike mechanic, enormous but cripplingly shy. The third to make up the group was a short, humble fellow, a gardener by trade, whose name nobody could ever quite remember. No one among the contestants, and no one in the crew. Not that he seemed to mind.

He's called ... Edwin? Osric? Manny thought. *No, erm ... Owen?*

(He was called Enwyn.)

Interview Excerpt

Interviewee: Enwyn

Age: 53

Appearance: Enwyn dresses in muted autumnal tones: coffee-coloured chinos and a comfy dark green cable-knit sweater. He's got a slightly receding hairline and short, scruffy, slightly curly hair. He speaks in a gentle, engaging Welsh lilt.

Enwyn: No, my dear fellow, it's *Enwyn*. Don't worry. Happens all the time. I don't mind at all.

[Listens to question from interviewer.]

Enwyn: Why will I win? Oh, I don't suppose I will. I'm not very special. I just applied for a bit of fun. I'm not a go-getting egomaniac like most of the people you see on television; we don't really get those in Wales, you see. I'm just a humble gardener!

[Listens to question again.]

Enwyn: Yes, there *is* something unique about me, I suppose. You see, when I was thirty-one, I got an infection that spread to my brain, and . . . [Claps loudly once.] That was it! I was in a coma for twenty years. When I woke up all of a sudden they thought it was a miracle. I thought things were all a bit modern and exciting in 2001. Now I'm constantly in a daze. Telephones you can watch movies on! Bit of an advance from my old rotary handset . . .

[Another question.]

Enwyn: Um, well, I've missed quite a lot: 9/11, a few popes, quite a lot of prime ministers. I've got a heck of a *Corrie* backlog. Then there's the scandals. Prince Andrew . . .

[Listens again.]

Enwyn: No, we always had our suspicions about Jimmy Savile. That did *not* come as a surprise.

Chapter Eleven

'What *happened*?' asked Cecil. 'How awful! Is he all right?'

They all looked from Cecil to the body. The awful right-angle that occurred in the middle of Yukio's neck, exactly at the point where, conventionally, necks are straight.

No one said anything.

'Stay calm, everyone,' said Manny, summoning some sort of authority into her voice. 'We'll get him the best care that we can. We just have to stay calm, okay? No more screaming.'

Reluctantly, she knelt next to Yukio's body.

She had not seen the final group approaching, from outside. Elliott, the grime DJ, Judith the housewife and the young blonde girl who had so unfairly accused Keith a few hours earlier of having murderous intentions. This last was an online influencer who called herself FlaymeZ.

Because Manny was kneeling, the new arrivals did not see the body until they were standing over it.

And when she saw it, FlaymeZ gave the loudest scream any of them had ever heard.

The scream echoed along the corridors, through the halls, up the stairwells, all the way through the castle.

'Oh, stop that,' said Manny. 'Get a hold of yourself.'

'But he's dead,' she said. 'He's actually dead. He's actually *really* dead!'

'Darling, don't be so ridiculous,' Manny said, with half a smile. 'This isn't real life. This is television.'

As she spoke she stroked the other woman's arm to calm her. With her other hand she put two fingers to the man's neck. Felt around. Felt some more.

Then under her breath she said the rudest word she knew.

He was actually, *really* dead.

Chapter Twelve

'This here is Inspector Constable,' said Millard, introducing the inspector to the chief medical officer, who was managing a team of others, as they tried to collect evidence without disturbing it.

'I won't shake hands,' said Dr Witt, through the face mask he wore beneath the whole-body white protective suit which was standard for major violent incidents. 'We're already up to our elbows here.'

'What can you tell me, doc?' Constable asked.

'This is a puzzle, and one that could take a long time to work out,' said Witt sharply. 'I'm not making empty promises about quick results. It's formidably complex – I think we've got several different incidents that occurred at separate times, which have cross-contaminated each other.'

He now pulled down his mask, revealing the lined face and harassed expression of someone doing an extremely difficult job in testing circumstances. 'It would help massively if we had mains electricity in the castle. One wonders how people survive like this.'

'Yes,' said Constable, looking around the room. 'Except I'm wondering how they *didn't* survive.'

'That is in questionable taste,' snapped the other man before turning to see that some of the other scene-of-crime officers were interested in what was being discussed. 'Okay, people, back to work! And be *ultra* cautious. I don't want anyone to move or to breathe without my say so!'

Inspector Constable thought his own remark was pretty acceptable. However, point-scoring would do nobody any good. And Witt was the most notoriously dour scene-of-crime expert in all of Scotland: a field that understandably had a great deal of competition.

'Anything you can tell me, any hints or suspicions (strong or otherwise) would be a help to me, when I interview the main witness in a few minutes' time,' said Constable. 'Then I might get information that could help you.'

Dr Witt did not acknowledge the validity of this assertion. He looked sourly over Constable's shoulder, clearly vexed at taking another moment away from analysing the pile of evidence he had to sort through.

'You see, the pressure's on me. And by extension, all of us,' said Constable. 'The media will be very interested in this case and will be asking for our response as soon as possible. So let's try and help each other if we can.'

Witt frowned, and actually met Constable's eyes for the first time in their discussion. 'I don't see why the media should be specially interested, or even aware yet . . .'

'The television show,' said Constable. He realised that there were no visible cameras about the place, no obvious accoutrements to tell anyone who came here that that is what had been going on.

Witt's eyes widened. He turned around, scanned the Mead Hall again as though for the first time. Saw the Dodecahedral Table.

'No way!' he said. 'No frigging way!'

'Er, yes, sir, this was the location for the filming . . .' put in PC Handcock.

'*The Faithfuls*! I love that show!' said Witt. 'OMFG, are you literally, literally kidding me?'

Inspector Constable tried to engage him in a few more words of conversation about the urgency of the task before them (which, in all fairness, Witt had already fully acknowledged), but he couldn't get a word in edgeways.

The pathologist was shouting to all the others in the room.

'Terry! Terry! Put that down for a sec! This is the set of the fucking *Faithfuls*, mate!'

Another all-over-white-suited figure in the middle distance dropped the dagger and blood-matted cloak he had been picking up.

'No bloody way,' he said. 'You're shitting me?'

'Karen!' said Dr Witt, and repeated his former statement. Yet another white-suited person appeared from behind the Dodecahedral Table, where she'd been hoovering crumbs into an evidence bag.

'I never twigged,' said Karen, looking around (with the exaggeratedly theatrical shoulder movements that were necessary when viewing the world from behind plastic glasses inside a full-body suit). 'Tell you what, some of these guys could have used a Shield, am I right?'

She laughed uproariously and slapped her side. Terry pointed at her and congratulated her, and kept repeating the comment to himself under his breath as though it was the cream of Wildean wit.

Inspector Constable was half bemused and two-thirds alarmed. He was rapidly recalibrating what this TV show was.

Of course, he had vaguely wondered whether the popularity of the programme might impede (or help) the investigation of what had happened here. But he had not until now quite appreciated the extent of that popularity. What other elements of the inquiry would that effect? The witness statements, the way people judged the severity of the crimes themselves, the potential motives?

Chapter Thirteen

'Okay, I need everyone to go into the games room straight away,' said an authoritative voice.

This shook them out of their reverie, and out of the stupefaction caused by that enormous scream which had vibrated along their spinal columns and made their heads rattle.

They all seemed to turn and look around to try to find out where the voice had come from.

Manny found herself staring at Judith. Who, aged about forty-five, was a quiet, serious little person. Liked by all who noticed her, which was by no means everyone. She was a housewife from Gloucester and she didn't make an awful lot of effort with her appearance (which made Manny find her adorable and innocent, like an injured vole). The only things Manny could really remember about her was that she was a pescetarian, a Presbyterian and the mother of two boys, one of whom had some sort of mental problem. *ADHD? ADD? ASD? AC/DC?*

'Okay,' Judith repeated. 'We've all had a minute to get to grips with this. Now please go into the games room. Manny, take his pulse.'

'I took it already,' Manny said.

'Do it again, please,' said Judith sternly.

The others ushered themselves towards the nearby games room, comforting each other, wondering aloud what could have happened.

Judith looked upwards.

'Well, he obviously fell,' she said. 'Have you got an ambulance on the way?'

'No, Judith, I only found him just a second ago—'

'You'd better ring now. Where's your phone? And how's that pulse?'

'Nothing,' said Manny sadly. She took out her phone with her spare hand and unlocked it. Then handed it over to Judith. *Where does all this natural authority come from?* she wondered.

'No signal,' said Manny. 'I'll try outside.'

'This is awful,' said Amina, who had been lurking nearby, giving off a vague sense that she thought she might be useful. 'I'll find a sheet,' she said.

'Where is everyone on the production team?' Judith asked, coming back in.

'Um, yeah, good question,' Manny answered. 'There's a slight chance there may be a storm coming. I don't think it was predicted by the weather forecast. That I know about, anyway.'

'But I asked where everyone is,' said Judith.

'It's a good question,' repeated Manny, still searching around on the dead man's neck and wishing she could be given permission to stop. 'We run a skeleton crew on this programme, to give people freedom to roam without feeling they're being watched, but this unexpected storm has made what staff we had go to the mainland.'

'Someone must have known about the storm,' said Judith. She was looking hard at Manny, who was pretending not to notice. 'It stands to reason.'

'The cows did,' said Manny. 'Because they were sitting down. But apparently it took everybody else by surprise.'

Judith overlooked this jumble of meaningless words as the sort of utterance that might escape someone suffering from extreme stress.

'What vehicles are there?' she asked.

Manny vaguely felt that there might be a cart or wagon in an outhouse somewhere on the grounds. And very possibly, somewhere in the fields nearby, a pony to which it might be hitched. That was probably their best bet. She decided not to say so.

'Manny,' said Judith, who then waited until Manny looked her in the eye. 'I think it's looking very likely that this man – it's the cameraman, isn't it? – has passed away. What's the protocol? There must be some very strict guidelines, and the procedure must be very well rehearsed.'

'Of course there are,' said Manny. She liked to maintain a level of charm even under direct challenge. But her civility was starting ever so slightly to slip under this interrogation.

'What are they then?' Judith asked.

'They're in there,' said Manny. She nodded at the pile of papers on the floor, which had half slid out of their folder when she had dropped it to examine Yukio. 'I haven't had a chance to read them yet.'

Judith nodded. 'I think you can stop taking his pulse now,' she said. Amina had returned with one of the distinctive cloaks worn by the Secret Murderers, which she'd found in a cupboard upstairs. 'Thank you, Amina,' Judith said, 'just lay it over right across the top. Yes, over the face as well. I'm afraid this site is the location of a serious death and will need to be investigated.'

She turned her head to look directly upwards. Amina and Manny did too.

The castle's entrance was also the heart of the building. Staircases ascended from the ground to the first and second floors, with ornately carved wooden galleries looking down.

There were paintings – portraits of dead dudes, mostly – weapons mounted on the walls, and deceased animals. Mostly the dead animals were heads with horns sticking out, but (as already noted) the taxidermists of the Scottish Highlands had also received lavish patronage from whatever posh nobs had been living here for the last (let's say) eight hundred years

Six feet above the three women was a colossal and magnificent chandelier. Two of the storeyed galleries came close to its edge. It was not obvious where Yukio had fallen from, but it had almost certainly been over one of the polished banisters that were nearly directly over their heads.

'Manny,' said Judith. Manny looked at her. She was still dazed. She didn't feel like she was going to stop feeling dazed any time soon. 'You've got to tell me what's going on.'

Police Interview Transcript

Interviewee: Manny Claudwinkle
Age: undetermined

Inspector Constable: Ms Claudwinkle, you've
got to tell me what's going on.

[Manuela Claudwinkle has been leaning on the
desk, staring down at her hands, possibly
asleep. When she looks up, her eyes are
bloodshot and red-rimmed. At least they
appear to be, under the large amount of
make-up.]

Claudwinkle: Oh, hi. Who are you?

Inspector: Inspector Constable, Highlands
Police. I'm investigating here.

[Claudwinkle shakes his offered hand.]

Claudwinkle: Excuse me for not getting up.

Inspector: Not at all. Thank you for talking to me.

Claudwinkle: Well. In the circumstances, inspector, it would be a bit rude to refuse. I expect you've got a question or two.

Inspector: There certainly does seem to be a little explaining to do. This is quite a situation.

[Claudwinkle sighs. She looks exhausted. She gathers herself and takes a deep breath.]

Claudwinkle: Well, it's a long story. I'll do my best . . .

Chapter Fourteen

M anny looked at her like she was mad. How could anyone tell what was going on?

'Um,' she said. 'Yes.'

Judith explained succinctly what she wanted to know. And Manny tried her best to answer with as little hesitation and stupidity as possible.

Where was the support?

There wasn't any.

Why?

Good question. The storm – the refusal of the taxi firm to drive today – the budget cuts.

Judith led her outside and they both looked at the sky. It was dark and threatening, looking like dusk even though it was barely past lunch. They both looked at Manny's phone – no signal. The wind was now blowing so hard they struggled to hear each other.

'So no one's coming? And we can't message the mainland?' Judith asked.

'Damian's definitely coming,' said Manny. 'But he won't have had a chance to get there and turn round yet.'

'And he doesn't know there's an emergency,' said Judith. 'Aside from the lack of cars. A real life-or-death emergency.'

It's not really a life-or-death emergency, Manny thought. *Just a death emergency.*

'Let's go in and talk to everyone,' said Judith.

Police Interview Transcript

Interviewee: Damian Shraw

Age: 54

Inspector Constable: So you were not able to return to the scene?

Damian Shraw: No — I really don't know if I'll ever be able to forgive myself for it. But in reality it would have been quite impossible. By the time I'd driven the ejected (and I suppose, quite naturally, *de*jected) contestant, Keith, back onto the mainland and to the nearest town, I had to drop him off at the hotel and see that he was okay. Then swing by the local office and check how things were before heading back.

Inspector: And you had to find some taxis.

Shraw: Yes, but that didn't worry me much.
As a producer I'm used to doing things over
the phone and sorting situations out on
the move. I decided to drive straight back
over to the island so Manny would have some
back-up but that's when I saw the other two
vehicles coming back the other way.

Inspector: [Flicks through notes.] So this
was the food truck and the make-up lady?

Shraw: Yes, Hassan the food guy, and Solaris
Benedicta. By the way, what a beautiful
name, don't you think?

Inspector: Is she involved in the rest of
the story of the day?

Shraw: Um — no, not at all.

Inspector: Then please proceed with what
happened next. Although yes, objectively I
can see it is a pleasant name.

Shraw: I'd stupidly spoken about the storm
in front of Hassan and Solaris. Who are
independent contractors, not employees of
mine in a strict sense ... [Thinks.] Well,
actually it was in their own interests
that they left, I suppose, in the long run.
So it's for the best. But I knew that the

people on the island didn't have food or
water. Which was a nightmare. All these
mistakes were adding up . . .

Inspector: Mistakes by who?

Shraw: I'm embarrassed to admit it. But . . .
there was a runner on the show. We hired
him out of a sense of duty, really. For
representation. We felt we were doing
the right thing. You see, he was a young
English white man. And at a team meeting
we recently realised we hadn't hired one of
those for about ten years. We were all a bit
embarrassed about it.

Inspector: And?

Shraw: It was a bit of a nightmare. He was
lazy and entitled, and didn't know what he
was doing but never admitted it. Things just
kept going wrong. I'm not attributing it to
his race — *I'd never do that*. But he was a
liability. He'd been supposed to keep the
castle stocked with bottled water, and he'd
forgotten, then gone off sick. I realised
that the people on the island would be
without water, which is . . .

Inspector: Certainly an inconvenience . . .

Shraw: Not to tell you your job, but I'm pretty sure it's against the law, inspector.

Inspector: That does sound about right. Although I'm murder, not workplace regulations.

Shraw: I drove out at once to the causeway, but even by then . . . the sea was at high tide, and the waves were already clearly over the road. I had to turn back. If I carried on, I could easily have got washed away.

Inspector: And drowned. Horrible.

Shraw: Yeah. Imagine the germs in that sea. Fish poo and shag and die in there. [Shudders.]

Chapter Fifteen

T he contestants were all sat around on chairs, on the floor, on the side of the pool table.

Someone had found a bottle of port in a decanter which was being poured for people. There was a murmur of disgust when it was discovered that the liquid within was only for show, and was actually flat Coca-Cola.

Louis the mechanic had gone in search of some more reviving liquor.

'I know that *The Faithfuls* often features people who have secret identities,' said Judith calmly, when everyone was sat (and Louis was pouring into proffered glasses from a purloined bottle of Viognier).

'We've all got to know each other very well in the last few weeks, and you thought I was a suburban yoga mum,' said Judith. 'In fact, until my second son was born, I was a detective inspector with the Somerset Police.'

There was a stir of interest at this.

'She lied to us,' FlaymeZ could be heard whispering.

Ignoring this, Judith then outlined the various facts as

she saw them, as succinctly as possible. The storm, the lack of access to emergency services . . .

'There's been an unspecified death at this address which will need to be investigated by the police. Not me – I don't belong to the local police force, and I'm not a working copper. But we need to keep things as undisturbed as possible. In fact, knowingly disturbing evidence is itself a crime. Well – it is in England, I'm pretty sure it must be under Scottish law too. So we've got to sit tight.'

'God, it's dark,' said Harry, who perhaps didn't like his wondrous jacket being less than perfectly visible to everyone. 'Elliott, can you switch the light on?'

Elliott was lounging in the doorframe. He nodded, and leant over to flick the switch. Nothing happened. He switched it again and again, with the same result.

Everyone was nonplussed.

'This castle has its own electricity supply, *surely*,' said Judith, turning to Manny.

Her words chimed with Manny's sentiments exactly. Surely it must! But this now appeared to be her responsibility.

'*Darling*,' said Manny. This was what she always said when she had no idea what to say next. It sounded like you had something to say. The pause that followed it also sounded deliberate and meaningful, the more so as the pause went on.

'Listen,' she said, which was a relatively transparent, but still sometimes effective, way of gaining an extra second of thinking time.

As she was starting to test the limits of the meaningful pause that could elapse before people would realise she had nothing to say and not a thought in her head, and was still fishing for words, someone else spoke up. It was Louis, the gentle giant.

'Um,' he said. 'I'm sorry to bother anyone. I don't want to cause any additional worry ...' He twiddled his fingers. 'But I just tried the tap in the kitchen. And nothing came out.'

Manny could feel the pack of printouts and information sheets under her arm, like it was some kind of beacon of shame. It seemed to vibrate and pulse like the floorboard concealing the tell-tale heart.

'You've all been drinking bottled water since you came here,' said Manny, realising as she said it that it was true. Not that she'd ever given this matter a second's thought before. 'Even at breakfast, when there are glass jugs, they've been filled by our wonderful caterer, Hassan.'

People were talking among themselves, looking at each other and glancing at Manny while she spoke. It annoyed her she couldn't hear what they were saying. And that they were not displaying the rigid fascination with her that they did when the cameras were rolling. She did not like the sensation.

'We can switch the water back on, though, yeah?' said Elliott.

'Darling,' said Manny. And thought furiously.

'Just be honest with us, Manny,' said Cecil. He was sitting back in an armchair and watching her over his glasses.

Until he said that, it actually hadn't occurred to Manny that she could be honest. It struck her as a novel twist.

'There never was any running water in the castle,' she said, finally tuning in to the memory of a speech she

73

remembered Damian giving to the production crew a few years earlier, when she'd been busy on her phone. But somehow, it seemed, still miraculously taking things in. 'Not since the Second World War, anyway, which was the last time it was fully occupied.'

Fiona, sat on the floor, asked with a sceptical air, 'So you put taps in for show?'

'For the cameras, yes,' said Manny.

Elliott flicked the light switch a few more times, getting everyone's attention. 'NO electricity,' he said.

The room focused on Manny again.

'The generator we use is connected to the catering van,' she said. 'The cameras run on batteries which last a full day. And – well – it's all to do with the way finances in the television industry work. You see, Hassan is on a zero-hours contracts, which means he and his van are not insured under our policy. Same with the make-up lady, that's why she's gone. . . .'

'Did you know what she's called?' Enwyn asked FlaymeZ.

'Oh, I know,' said FlaymeZ.

'Solaris Benedicta,' said Fiona wonderingly.

'*Such* a beautiful name,' agreed Cecil.

Manny agreed vociferously, but saw that the demand for her full explanation wasn't going to be so easily derailed. 'So, Hassan's vehicle is the only one large enough to tow the generator here every day, from the mainland . . .'

'We don't care about the finances,' Harry said quietly. 'Sorry to be rude. But what we want to know is – there's no electricity or water in this place?'

'And no food,' said Fiona.

'I'm sure there's some bottled water,' Manny said. Then realised this was not good enough. 'No,' she admitted.

But there's definitely a nut bar around the place somewhere.

'And we're stuck here until the storm ends?' said FlaymeZ.

Manny looked to Judith – who had miraculously been revealed as a responsible adult, rather than the gormless yoga mum she had seemed until now to be – for help. Judith was visibly unamused by being used as back-up. It was certainly not her fault, after all.

'In the high seas caused by a storm, it would definitely be a bad idea to try and leave,' she said. 'The causeway is too narrow. Real risk of death.'

They all went quiet. But the castle didn't. There was the rattling of window shutters, heard from all over the building, and the sound of the wind, which growled and moaned, and was starting to howl.

'Who killed Yukio, then?' asked FlaymeZ.

Police Interview Transcript

Interviewee: Manny Claudwinkle

Age: undetermined

Inspector Constable: I'm very interested to hear your account of what happened at the castle. However, first I'm interested to know why you came up with this game.

Claudwinkle: I didn't come up with diddly squat, inspector. I never have in my life. Except my kids. And even they are both more productive and creative than me — all I can produce to this day is a fair plate of scrambled eggs. [Pause.] It was a pair of geniuses in Belgium who invented the thing, as far as I'm aware. Clever buggers. Clever *rich* buggers.

Inspector: I'm sure, but what I'm asking is: why do you like it?

Claudwinkle: Because it's brilliant. It's hugely popular, everyone who watches it adores it. It's ... Well, I was going to say 'crack cocaine' but I feel funny saying that in front of a police inspector.

Inspector: Have you ever taken crack cocaine?

Claudwinkle: [Sighs.] *No*. But thanks for asking. [Pause.] Have you?

Inspector: I have not. There haven't been any violent deaths in the Belgian version of this game, then?

Claudwinkle: I don't suppose so. Or I'm sure I'd have heard of them. It's been sold all over the world. There were some rumours of funny goings on in the Romanian version, which was set in a castle in Transylvania, but that may be horseshit. Or rather *bat*shit. Why are different types of shit given human characteristics, do you think? Is pigshit stupid, batshit crazy, or dogshit somehow worth less than other kinds?

[Inspector Constable regards her for a while, sips coffee, clears throat.]

Claudwinkle: But you think I'm talking bullshit.

Inspector: You didn't think there was anything dangerous or risky about having these people together and encouraging them to suspect each other of murder?

Claudwinkle: Oh, heavens. Don't you watch reality TV?

Inspector: I watch the news, that's reality. Does that count?

Claudwinkle: You're being silly. I mean *Big Brother*, *Survivor*, *The Apprentice*.

Inspector: Tell me about these.

Claudwinkle: You *can't* be serious?

Inspector: We are after all in a police interrogation room discussing several unexplained deaths.

Claudwinkle: So it would be fair to assume you're always being serious. Fine. You haven't seen any of them. Okay. So, *Survivor* is about people left alone to fend for themselves on a desert island with no assistance, to see if they can survive.

Big Brother is about people trapped within essentially a small prison being watched over by an evil eye that sees everything they do. And *The Apprentice* shows deluded young people clambering over each other to get a chance to be hired by — well, in the American version, it was Donald Trump.

Inspector: [Clearly disturbed.] This all sounds . . . *very* . . .

Claudwinkle: Is it not patently obvious that all of those situations would be extremely entertaining to watch?

Inspector: To an ingrained sadist, I think, perhaps. And they don't, I assume — tell me if I'm wrong — usually end up with dead bodies?

Claudwinkle: Ignoring that last remark for a moment — they are all masterpieces of entertainment. You're missing out if you deny yourself them. What do you watch?

Inspector: That's not germane to this discussion.

Claudwinkle: Humour me, inspector. Let's have a bit of back-and-forth. You watch something for entertainment? Something with some real human content?

Inspector: [Considers.] I suppose I don't mind watching the snooker. When it's on.

Claudwinkle: Nothing could be more chilling and cold blooded.

Inspector: Speaking of which, hopefully you can tell me what happened next . . .

Chapter Sixteen

'It's thoroughly irresponsible to start speculating about Yukio's death,' said Judith. 'It was almost certainly an accident. But we can't find that out ourselves. Until the storm stops, and help arrives.'

'Yukio had a phone though,' said Manny.

Everyone looked at her. She held her own phone up. 'Mine's rubbish,' she said. 'We just tried it. But his might be better, could get a signal. Then we might be able to get help.'

Judith, until today so quiet, so meek, was now absolutely in charge. 'Everyone stay here,' she said. 'Amina and Manny, you've already been near the body, so come with me ...'

They went back to the hall and Manny squeamishly recovered Yukio's phone from within his jeans pocket. For some reason being beneath a sheet made the body more of an object of fear and revulsion than if it had been fully exposed.

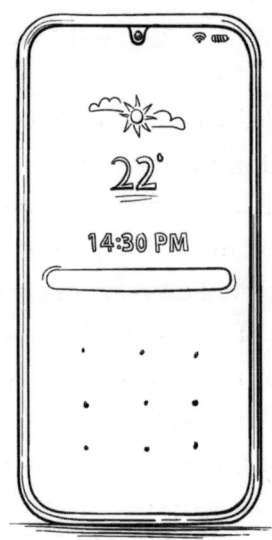

'Hold his finger to it,' said Amina, when she saw that the password was fingerprint controlled. It worked. 'Fetch me his laptop?' she added.

Manny went to find Yukio's computer, which needed to be on site to control and record the input from the cameras. It was in an otherwise disused alcove on the first-floor gallery in the entrance hall. Manny knew he liked to sit there, because it was a spot safe from the glance of the cameras and meant he wouldn't accidentally get in a shot and ruin it. It added credence to the idea that it must have been from somewhere around this place that he had fallen.

She brought the computer back downstairs to the games room, where everyone watched Amina do her magic. Naturally the laptop was locked. But after tapping at the keyboard and switching it on and off a few times, she was working away at it, with apparent full access.

'How did you do that?' Harry asked, watching over her shoulder.

'Trick of the trade,' said Amina. 'I'm in IT support. You normos are always fouling up your computers and getting into all sorts of trouble. We professionals need to be able to get in and sort out your . . . My god, what's this?'

Others came and looked over her shoulder, their faces showing a mixture of fear and admiration at her ability to gain access. The admiration quickly turned to confusion and disgust, however, as they realised what they were looking at.

Amina had found the programme that showed the view from all the cameras, sorted on the screen into tiles. There were the obvious ones: the corridor, the games room, the library, the Mead Hall.

'But look here,' said Amina quietly. The cursor hung over an internal view of a small featureless cubicle. It looked like a toilet. And the next tile along showed another similar space.

'That's the gents' Portakabin,' said Harry, shocked. 'What's he want a camera in there for?'

'And that's the ladies',' said Fiona. 'Sick bastard. And look – that's the shower!' She and Harry exchanged a look. Then they both did the same with their other near neighbours. Elliott and Louis and Harry, Cecil and Enwyn the gardener, FlaymeZ and Amina. Judith and Manny glanced at each other, aware this was getting more serious by the moment.

'If he's been recording people when they're naked,' said Harry, 'and someone found out . . .'

'They'd be pretty pissed off,' said Fiona. 'I mean, *I* would be. Anyone would be!'

Manny desperately wanted a lie down, a massage and a Cornetto. A thought in the back of her mind was trying to form, but it was so exhausting that she couldn't put it into words.

'Fuck me,' she said. 'If I found that out about him, I'd *murder* the fucker.'

From the corner of her eye, she saw Judith nodding.

Police Interview Transcript

Interviewee: Damian Shraw

Age: 54

Shraw: Actually, as it happens, we don't
select people for the show based on how
mad and insecure they are. I appreciate
it might look like that sometimes. But the
truth is quite the opposite. It just so
happens that when you put ordinary people
in a stressful situation and they're on
screen, strange things happen. They become
other people, they change. It's chimerical,
it's magical, it's sometimes embarrassing,
sometimes brilliant — that's what makes TV
so entertaining.

Inspector Constable: Except when people get
actually killed as a consequence, perhaps.

[Awkward pause.]

Shraw: Yes. That's a good point. Yes, except
for then.

Chapter Seventeen

Judith and Manny had to shout to get everyone to calm down.

But whenever it got quiet enough to hear again, some-one started shouting.

'Are you saying,' said Fiona, when the vocal storm had subsided long enough to hear the storm outside, 'that one of us might be a murderer?'

There was a moment of miraculous, stunned silence at this. The irony was pretty unignorable, but thankfully no one actually laughed.

'Let's not leap to conclusions,' said Judith. 'There's no reason to think that.'

'Except for a strong motive,' said Cecil.

'And a violent death,' added Elliott.

'As Judith says, let's not jump to conclusions,' said Manny. 'Pun not intended. Too soon? Too soon.'

'If Amina broke into his computer this time, why couldn't she have done it before?' asked FlaymeZ.

'Why on earth would she have done that?' said Judith.

'To get a view on what's going on round here. Listen in

to people through the cameras?' said FlaymeZ. 'I mean, this is a pretty amazing secret skill, right?'

'I'm an IT consultant,' said Amina. 'It's one of the most common jobs in the world – it's hardly a secret skill. Doesn't make me a ninja. Besides, what would I know about TV cameras and how they work? I thought it was all relayed back to a studio somewhere.'

'Oh yeah,' said FlaymeZ. 'So did I. That's a good point actually.'

'But here we are in this faraway place, in the middle of nowhere,' said Cecil, looking at everyone over steepled fingers from within the comfy depths of his armchair. 'And this whole show is about secret identities. What if one of those identities . . .'

'Is murderer?' said Elliott. 'But we all volunteered to be Murderers, Cecil!'

Ideally, Manny thought, *I would get people to stop using the word murderer right now. How exactly am I going to go about that?*

'I think this is distasteful,' said Harry the artist. He stood up and took a few paces. 'Let's not *speculate* that people have secret identities . . .'

Manny, watching him so discomfited, instinctively cast an eye across all the contestants. She saw them exchanging looks. And thinking . . . *here's something. Let's make a note of this* . . .

'Well, we already know about Samantha and Jasper,' said Elliott. 'Who would have predicted those two being together?'

'Yeah, that was quite the age gap,' said Cecil. 'She was older than me, for goodness sake.'

'Good on her, I say,' said Fiona. 'Get in there, lass.'

'Can I point out, my lovelies,' Manny said, 'that we need to consider something carefully. The fact that we definitely know there's at least one Murderer in the room?'

Chapter Eighteen

'I'll leave you to it then,' said Inspector Millard, the local police chief. 'I think you're mostly caught up on everyone you need to meet.'

Inspector Constable shook his hand tightly. Inspector Millard's hair was doing that thing again, because they were standing in the backdraft of yet another police helicopter. This one was preparing to take Millard back to the pleasant quiet of his local station, Constable thought, with considerable envy.

The storm which had struck in the past two days had decimated the causeway between the island and the mainland. When the seas and the winds retreated, they had left a road that one could only just about detect, visually. It looked like a child's drawing that had been half rubbed out. No one would approve a vehicle to drive over it, so it was helicopter taxis for everyone.

'Listen, Jim,' said Constable, as they watched the chopper getting ready. 'I've not had a chance to ask anyone else. What is this programme, exactly?'

Millard was so obviously anticipating getting out of the

place, that he looked inconvenienced at having to consider one final work question.

'It's a murder mystery,' he said.

'Right.'

'Where people kill each other in a castle until there's hardly any of them left.'

'Okay.'

'To win money. Well, so long then!' And with a hop and a skip, the local sheriff jumped up into the empty seat and shut the door behind him.

Constable turned back to the castle, with several more questions on his lips. But he just looked at the battered exterior, with so many windows shattered, and storm damage visible on every side.

It seemed kind of like Agatha Christie's *And Then There Were None*, which (his wife was an aficionado of such things) he had read while they were on holiday in Thessaloniki one year and actually made him skip his pork gyro at dinner. Why did people make up such things for entertainment? What (he had wondered then, and wondered again now with renewed force) if somehow imagining such a thing made it *come true*?

He knew there was always a danger that he was being stupid and too literal.

But it seemed to him there was a chance that someone had taken the game too seriously.

Chapter Nineteen

At Manny's suggestion there was a murderer in their midst, the emotional temperature in the room grew three degrees colder.

Which was the same direction the physical temperature was going too. Storm rain was now pattering on the windows in irregular bursts, like handfuls of gravel thrown by half-hearted schoolboys.

'I'm talking about the show,' Manny said.

Around the room, shoulder muscles relaxed.

'Obviously the show will have to go on hiatus while this is investigated,' Manny said. 'But afterwards, can it continue?'

'Of course it can,' said FlaymeZ.

'No reason why not,' said Cecil, 'surely?'

'As long as it's done in a way that's respectful to the family,' said Louis the mechanic. 'I mean, I assume it would be ... what he wanted?'

Manny looked around the room. Her heart swelled. These people loved the show as much as she did. And she loved them. None of them yet realised that if this series came off the air – that was it. The production company would pocket the insurance money, breathe a sigh of relief and cancel the whole thing in the same breath.

'I don't want to lead anyone,' she said. 'But if any of you reveal to each other that you are a Murderer in the show, there's no show. Cat and bag no longer on speaking terms. All over.'

Despite the fact they were in the presence of violent death, this got everyone's attention.

They all still wanted to be on TV. The idea of that going away because of some stupid accident was horrifying. Tantalising.

Even Judith had a light of temptation in her eyes. But with a visible effort, she controlled it.

'That's ridiculous,' Judith said. 'Just forget about the TV show right now. It's not important. I don't want people talking about accusing each other of murder for some game, when there's a chance that we're at the site of a real murder. TV is not as important as life.'

There was an uncomfortable silence.

A few people looked at each other.

'So you think it *could* be a murder then?' asked Fiona, the word *murder* purring in her Glaswegian accent.

'I'm not thinking about that,' Judith snapped. She looked out of sorts – maybe the stress was getting to her – blinking rapidly, and swallowing. 'It's not for me to say. They'll have to look into it. For now, we all stay in this room, *don't* talk about murder, and don't do *anything* that might put any of us in danger.'

They all nodded.

She raised the cup of tea she'd been cradling in both hands and took a sip.

The stress really *was* getting to her; Manny noticed that she was starting to shiver.

Poor thing needs a hug, Manny thought. But before she could get up and go over, Judith's shivering became more pronounced. She seemed to lose her balance, slopped the tea on the carpet, and then fell to the floor.

'My god, what's wrong?' asked Cecil. 'Someone help her!'

Elliott jumped across the room and knelt beside her.

'I know first aid,' he said.

She was shaking uncontrollably. Others stood over her and offered advice as Elliott tried to stop her from biting her tongue off. Shockingly fast, she went still. They saw a white foam drooling from her lips.

Elliott was holding her wrist. He looked up desperately.

'She's dead,' he said.

Police Interview Transcript

Interviewee: Manny Claudwinkle

Age: undetermined

Inspector Constable: So, was it at this moment you started to think that there could actually be a murderer in the group? And not just talking about the show, I mean.

Claudwinkle: No, inspector, because I'm not insane. You're looking at this through the eyes of someone who knows what happened later. I did *not* know what was going to happen later. I very much wanted to stop people panicking and distressing themselves, after two horrible accidents. Incidents. Accidents. [She hesitates.] . . . *But.*

Inspector: But what?

Claudwinkle: At first something stopped me really getting a grip on the situation. It was something Damian, the producer, had said. Months earlier. At the end of a meeting, when we were going back to our cars, just before filming was about to start.

Inspector: He said . . .

Claudwinkle: He said, 'How would you feel if there was a genuine murderer in the castle with you?'

Inspector: And what did he mean by that?

Claudwinkle: Now that, inspector, is a bloody good question. At the time, I was tired, and I thought he was trying to be funny, and just managing to be a bit of a tit.

Inspector: Is he the sort of person who likes to try to be funny?

Claudwinkle: Absolutely not. He is the least funny individual I've ever met in my life. As it happens. I ignored him when he said it. But possibly that's exactly why it came back to me at that moment, when what happened to Judith . . . *happened* to Judith.

Inspector: Do you think you know what he meant now?

Claudwinkle: Of course. Later, someone opened their mouth and cleared up the whole mystery . . .

Chapter Twenty

FlaymeZ burst into tears and threw herself against the nearest person – who happened to be Cecil. He looked startled and held her rather stiffly, patting the top of her head.

'Don't worry, dear,' he said.

'Feels like maybe we *ought* to worry,' said Fiona. She touched the cup with the toe of her shoe. 'Where did that cup of tea come from? I didn't see her make it.'

They all shook their heads. None of them could remember anyone offering to make a cup, or bringing it.

'This is awful,' said Manny. 'Let's try and catch our breaths.'

Elliott was still energetically trying to resuscitate Judith, and getting more and more desperate. Enwyn put his hand softly on Elliott's shoulder and he seemed to realise that there was nothing more he could do.

'Obviously I love you guys,' FlaymeZ was saying. 'Meeting you has been the most amazing experience of my life. I adore you all. All of you. I mean it. And I trust you with my life . . .'

The others, scattered around the games room in groups, all nodded their heads sincerely.

'But,' she went on, 'it's looking pretty obvious to me that there's an actual murderer here.'

'Someone in this room?' said Amina, looking round.

'Now, let's try and keep things calm,' said Manny. 'Don't jump to conclusions . . .'

'It's impossible,' said Fiona. 'I know you guys. I know you'd never, ever want to do anything like that.'

'Except that we all volunteered to go on a show in the hope that we'd get picked as Murderers,' said Enwyn.

'But not *for real*, Owen,' said Elliott.

'It's Enwyn,' said Enwyn.

'Right – sorry. Sorry, Enwyn.'

'That's okay. Happens all the time.'

'I love you, man.'

'You too!' For some reason the little Welshman couldn't keep a small smile from his face. Possibly it was nerves, thought Manny, but it was unnerving everyone else all the same.

'Isn't that suspicious?' FlaymeZ asked. 'That he just said that? I'm sorry – I love you,' she said, reaching out a hand to pat Enwyn's arm. 'I'd never suspect you. You are a true Faithful. One hundred per cent. It's just . . . well, if anyone was going to have access to poison . . .'

The word seemed to whisper poisonously in the supremely suggestible ears of everyone who heard it, who all turned to look at the body. They all, including Manny, thought the same, damning thought, and it was not an accusation of Enwyn. But a far more threatening possibility . . .

'You don't think,' said FlaymeZ. 'That it could be ...'

'Surely not,' said Cecil.

'But she did admit she was one ...' Elliott could not prevent himself from saying.

Interview Excerpt

Interviewee: Brenda

Age: 61

Appearance: Brenda is sensibly dressed and serious looking, in a pale blue blouse with a ruched collar and an ebony brooch.

Brenda: Yes, I don't make any bones about being a witch. It's not something I particularly want to keep secret. I am one, that's that. Part of the reason I'm so up front is that being a witch isn't exactly what people expect. You see, I'm a health practitioner; I run a practice. If anything, I spend most of my time interviewing people, paying invoices, speaking to suppliers, being on the local board of shopkeepers, making sure the street looks smart and so on. The idea that I spend any of my spare

time putting pins through wicker figures of
people and burying them under a full moon
is frankly insulting and anyone who suggests
such nonsense will have me to answer to.
Childish rubbish! Yes, I'll have a coffee and
a pink wafer, thank you . . .

**FATE ON *THE FAITHFULS*: KILLED BY THE
MURDERERS — EPISODE SIX**

Chapter Twenty-one

'Nah,' said Elliott, after a moment.

'Yeah, he's right: "nah",' said Fiona. 'What were we thinking?'

'That woman was the closest to an accountant a witch could possibly be,' said Manny, relieved to find the consensus swinging in the direction of sanity.

Unless she was mistaken in her train of thought, for a moment there they had all been thinking that a former contestant had returned to the island and staked them out in order to commit murder, which was the next level down in the dungeon of paranoia.

But then, how many layers of paranoia were there? The night was young.

Her heart was beating desperately.

'At least Brenda was open about what she was,' said Fiona. 'I mean – after all, there's the other thing we're all thinking ... That we know several of us have got secrets.'

'No secret about that,' said Fiona stonily, eyeing her fellow contestants, who either stared her down defiantly or looked shifty.

'Maybe we should reveal them now,' said Cecil briskly. 'Get it over with.'

There was another uncomfortable silence.

The TV show is lost now, for sure, Manny thought.

In fact she was thinking faster than she ever had in her life. Her brain was working away like a mad thing, making rapid calculations.

We could replace Judith with one of the people knocked out in a former round, she thought. *That could work. Alternatively we could re-cast the Secret Murderers from this point onwards and start the game again from a smaller cast. Would that work? Wouldn't it lose all the tension that had been built up with the previous cast of Murderers?*

She thought it *might* work, but slightly less satisfactorily than the usual recipe.

Then, guiltily, looking down at Judith's still form, she realised she was a cold and calculating monster. Not faithful in the slightest. Stop worrying about bloody television, Manny. 'No reason not to reveal who you are,' she said. 'Who goes first?'

Rain was falling in torrents. The windows were creaking and groaning in the wind.

'I'll go first,' said Cecil. 'I know that I told you all I was a businessman, but in fact I'm a, a councillor, an elected politician. And, actually, the party I represent is Reform UK.'

There was a bit of a shudder in the room, and FlaymeZ, who had been standing next to him, took a step back. Elliott looked disgusted, Amina looked alarmed, and Fiona's face took on a stone-like hardness. Which wasn't far from how it looked normally, to be fair, but it became overshadowed by a noticeably more rugged and unfriendly expression.

'I know that's not the most popular position to have. But there you are – that's what I do. Who's next?'

But everyone wanted a minute to take this in.

'I think we shouldn't talk over Judith's body like this, it feels disrespectful,' said Manny. The others agreed.

'There's one other room we could go to,' she said. 'Where we could be safe. Away from the windows, which might break.'

Police Interview Transcript

Interviewee: Manny Claudwinkle

Age: undetermined

Inspector Constable: Only one other room you could go to? In a whole castle?

Claudwinkle: That's the thing. The castle looks pretty from the outside, but on the inside it's mostly unsafe. It's a thousand years old, for Pete's sake. It's used for movie and TV-show exteriors, but they've only managed to make four rooms at the front of the castle liveable.

Inspector: So what's the other room, then, that you went to?

Claudwinkle: Well, I was desperate that they
stop thinking that this was some kind of
fictional murder mystery brought to life.
So seeing as we were trapped inside a large
house in a storm, I got them all to assemble
in the library so I could give a speech I
wanted everybody to hear . . .

Chapter Twenty-two

'There'll be *no more talk* about murders,' Manny was saying. 'Just because there's been two horrible accidents, I don't want this to get out of hand.'

No one said anything.

They were sat on chairs and couches in the plushly decorated library. A fire ought to have been burning in the grate but, unlike the actual roaring logs in the Mead Hall, it was in fact an LCD screen with a picture of a fire in it. Which meant that right now it was a blank grey space.

Instead, the room was lit with candles, which they'd found with great relief in the drawer of a kitchen dresser.

'Is that clear?' she asked sternly.

They all looked thoroughly tired and frightened. Scared for their lives. Except for Angwyn – or was it Emlyn? – who was still smiling his discreet little smile.

Funny little man.

'We should take our minds off it,' said Manny. 'Let's talk about something else.'

'Tell stories,' said Cecil.

'Ghost stories,' said Fiona.

'No, *not* ghost stories,' said Manny.

'Play a game, then,' said Louis.

'Cluedo,' said Eowyn, smiling.

'Not *Cluedo*!' Manny said. 'Come *on*, guys!'

'Game-playing is good for stress relief,' said FlaymeZ. 'And social bonding. It builds and strengthens relationships across class divides and social boundaries.'

'Very wise words,' said Cecil.

'It's written on the back of this Jenga box,' said FlaymeZ.

This is more like it, Manny told herself. *Let them chat. Keep them chatting.*

She put her hand on a table beside her, and felt a slip of paper.

'What's that in your hand?' Fiona asked.

Manny looked over the top of it, at them.

'Um, nothing,' she said.

'What is it?' Amina said.

'It's nothing,' said Manny. It was too late. She couldn't hide it. She wanted to stuff it down her top or preferably burn it. But the nearest candle was too far away.

She just stood there like a lemon and held it, wavering slightly, until Louis stood up to reassure her, as she was looking frail. He looked at it.

'Oh ... *sugar,*' he said.

Police Interview Transcript

Interviewee: Manny Claudwinkle

Age: undetermined

Inspector Constable: And what was written
on it?

Claudwinkle: [She holds out her hands and
pinches the air as though she's got the
paper in them.] It was a little envelope, the
sort you'd get a save-the-date in, or the
message that comes with a bunch of flowers.
Inside was a slip of paper, and on it was
written in ink, by hand, 'All of you are
guilty. Only one of you will survive.'

Inspector: I see. And how did you react
to that?

Claudwinkle: Now, you see *that*, inspector, if you don't mind me saying, is a positively *stupid* question.

Chapter Twenty-three

'We're all going to die,' said Amina. 'I knew it. I've felt it all day . . .'

'Calm down,' said Manny half-heartedly.

'There's a murderer here. One of you!' said FlaymeZ.

'I trust you all. You're a hundred per cent faithful. It *can't* be one of you. I know it isn't!' Elliott said.

'Where were you when we were in the games room, Louis?' Harry asked. 'I'm sorry to say it – I just don't re-member seeing you there. After you handed round the wine, I mean.'

'I was there,' said Louis quietly. He seemed to stoop, to shrink into himself under everyone's gaze.

'But I saw you coming back into the room, a few min-utes before Judith died,' said Fiona. 'Even though I'd not seen you go out.' Everyone went quiet. 'I'm sorry, hun, you know I love you. But I'm scared right now . . .'

'I didn't . . . I . . . I went to the bathroom.' Louis was a tremendous figure of a man, with broad shoulders and wonderful muscle mass. But, always pale and shy, he now looked almost crushed by this sudden suspicion.

In fact, Manny thought to herself, *I think this is the first time I've ever actually seen someone cower. It was always just a word to me before.*

'So why did you lie?' Elliott asked him.

'I didn't! I mean, I didn't think, think it mattered – it was just a trip to the bathroom.'

It was pathetic and horrible to watch. Manny wished she could bring a stop to it.

'The cup of tea was already in Judith's hand when I came back in,' insisted Louis – but feebly.

'It's just, it looks bad that you lied, Loo,' said FlaymeZ. 'What can we think—'

'I've just thought of something,' said Cecil. 'The armoury. Where the Shield is hidden. There are weapons in there, on the wall.'

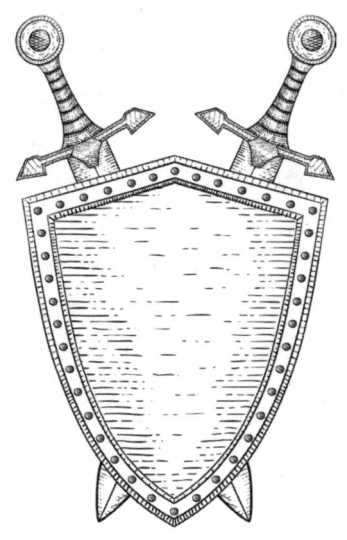

'They're fake, just imitations,' said Fiona.

'I don't care about that. I can defend myself with a

fake sword nearly as well as a real one … Better than nothing …'

Manny reached out and put a reassuring hand on Louis's arm, pretty sure (although it was hard to tell in the candle-light) that he was trembling with tears.

'We should *not* go to the armoury,' said Manny. 'We should stay here.'

She gave everyone the sternest glance she could muster, but it was powerless in the murky dimness. So hard to make any-thing out – except she saw to her disbelief that Enron was now smiling more than ever. He had a positive twinkle in his eyes!

If he wasn't absolutely the most innocent person Manny had ever met, she would have been convinced he was trying to tell her something. Something sinister.

He still thinks this is all a game, she suddenly realised. *That it's all pretend. Oh, thank god. Let him carry on thinking that!*

'All this sensible advice has only got us into more danger. We don't know who wrote that note, but they've said spe-cifically that they want to kill us all,' said Elliott. 'There are shields in there too.'

'I'd sleep safer with a shield,' said Harry.

The room all agreed they'd sleep safer with a shield.

I bloody wouldn't, thought Manny, *but then I'm starting to think I'll never sleep again.*

Manny could feel that she was losing the last of her con-trol over this group. She felt dizzy.

'*Please* stay here,' she said. But they were all getting up and fetching candles.

She didn't want to stay in the library on her own, so she followed them out into the corridor. She wanted to beg them to come back.

'Stay together!' she said. And she wanted to add, *Please! It's for your own good! I just want you to be safe!* But she knew such maternal admonitions were always ignored, or even counterproductive.

'It's through here!' came a voice from further down the corridor. There was a distant clattering noise, an indistinct human sound.

'My god, it's proper dark outside already and it's not even five,' said Harry.

They heard the tinkle of breaking glass somewhere in the distance and the sound of the wind got suddenly louder. A window blown in, or shattered by something catapulted on the storm.

'I think it's this way,' said Cecil, turning with a candle in his hand to talk to those behind him. 'I didn't see which way the guys ahead went . . .'

'No, look,' said Louis. 'We're practically in the Mead Hall. Go back . . .'

But they had all realised that there were weapons on the wall of the Mead Hall, too.

As they went in, they saw there was a strange shape in front of the fire. It took Manny a moment to tell what it was.

My god . . .

It was Elwyn. (Olwyn? Osmond?) The enormous medieval pike which had been hanging magisterially on the wall above the fire had fallen from its place on the wall.

Its blade had pierced right through him, pinning him to the floor.

He wasn't moving.

And he wouldn't be any time soon, either.

115

Chapter Twenty-four

After touching base with all the key staff members, a picture was starting to form in Inspector Constable's mind. *Far* from a complete one, however. Very much at the early pencil-sketch stage – a join the dots with two thirds of the dots yet to be applied.

But it was not good. This was going to be a big story and probably declared a serious major incident.

He had to call his boss, the detective chief superintendent. He'd only ever had to do this once before, when dealing with a Hollywood actor who'd been in a fatal collision while under the influence. You only wanted to do it under the most severe, direst circumstances, and when there was no other option.

The detective chief superintendent was not known as Vesuvius just because he was ancient, red-faced and as hard as rock. He was said to play tennis without a racquet, returning the ball across the court just by shouting.

Not that he had the appearance of a keen tennis player, exactly. Unless there was a bar at the club perhaps. In physical terms . . . well, Vesuvius suited him on a number of levels.

Most of all, of course, being his reaction to bad news . . .

Constable looked at his phone. Looked out across the windswept countryside for a moment and took a deep breath. Rehearsed in his mind all the key phrases that you needed to use when there was a giant mess and you had absolutely diddly squat idea of what was going on.

He dialled.

The call connected. He identified himself and asked to speak to the chief, and when he heard the click, drove straight on with his account of what they knew so far.

'My god,' said a female voice, 'you're *so brave*?'

'Detective chief superintendent?' he asked.

'That sounds horrible. Poor you. How are you feeling?'

'Um, excuse me,' said Constable. 'It's a difficult line, all the way out here. May I speak to the detective chief superintendent?'

'Yeah!' said the voice. 'DCS Totterill speaking!'

'Ah,' said Constable. 'So DCS Leaming is . . .'

'He retired on Friday. Good timing, eh? Clever sausage that he is! Tootling off to the golf course, no doubt . . .'

'If the golf course has a bar, perhaps,' said Constable, almost to himself.

'Oh my god, you are *so funny*,' said Totterill. 'In the face of such death and horror. I admire you. I do! I *admire* you.'

He remembered her now. Of course they had met, many times – it had taken him a minute to place her.

Constable felt slightly off-kilter, as the energy he'd stored up for what had threatened to be a colossal confrontation-cum-conflagration swilled around inside him. He gave a concise-ish explanation of what he knew so far, staying very guarded and official.

Given the tone of the conversation, he felt rather like a mouse eyeing a piece of cheese and trying to work out where the trap mechanics were hidden.

'Do you think we still have a killer at large?' was the question she asked next. 'Sorry to be all official-y.'

'I would say this is the most complex scenario I've yet encountered,' he admitted. 'There has been dramatic loss of life, in strange circumstances, but it is very hard to tell intent or culpability at this stage. Obviously the media will be interested and we will have to release what we know soon. I'll interview the main person of interest presently, and then we should have a clearer picture. I'll report back to you at once.'

'Looking forward to it!' said DCS Totterill. 'And *look after yourself*, okay? Missing you already!'

Chapter Twenty-five

'I feel like I've known you all my life,' said Harry, candle-light glinting off his huge, brick-like glasses. 'I trust you all. You've all had such an effect on me. I've never met a group who make me feel so accepted, so loved.'

Manny was glad to hear him say it.

The effect of his words was mitigated, however, by the fact he was saying them through the lowered visor of a knight's helmet. He clutched a wooden staff from which hung a spiked ball. It was made of cast iron, and wobbled in his hand as he tried to hold it up. Possibly from the sincerity of the emotions of friendship and loyalty he was expressing.

'I feel the same,' said Cecil. 'I love how different we all are – geographically, socially, age-wise – and the fact that we'd never ordinarily have met each other. And formed such friendships ...' He was backed up into a corner behind an armchair, protecting himself with a duelling sword.

'Could literally not have put it better myself,' said FlaymeZ, her voice somewhat smothered by the chainmail she'd pulled over her head and was still trying to adjust. Her eyes emerged from the aperture and swivelled nervously. In her spare hand was a bow, and a quiver of arrows was by her feet.

'I don't believe it,' said Amina.

'You've never trusted me from the start,' said FlaymeZ. 'You've always had a problem with me! I don't know what it is! And I love you so much – but ...'

'No – not that,' said Amina. 'FlaymeZ, mate – listen. *I just got a bar of signal.*'

'On what?' Manny asked. No devices, of course, were allowed on the castle grounds. It was a very strict rule to remove the temptation of skulduggery or cheating, and to force people to talk rather than be on their phones. She was fascinated more than aggrieved.

'Smuggled it in in my sock,' said Amina, holding up a smartphone. 'I've been checking it to see if I could get a signal. Just one bar and it was gone in a second.'

'If we *can* tell people what's happened,' said Fiona. 'Then we have to, as quick as possible.'

'All our lives are at stake,' said Harry. 'Try and get that one bar back!'

Amina gave him an exasperated look.

'Well, I don't know, go in different directions until you see it again,' Harry said defensively.

Manny opened her mouth to tell them that this was a bad idea, but they were already at the door, lumbering and clambering with their heavy weapons. She put a hand over her eyes and took a long breath.

Soon there were hoots of victory from the corridor outside. The signal had fleetingly returned.

'It's coming from the front,' they reported. 'We're going outside.'

'Wait just one minute,' said Manny. 'It's incredibly dangerous out there.'

'But our lives might depend on finding this signal,' said Elliott.

'There's a killer who's told us that only one of us will survive,' said FlaymeZ, quite reasonably (albeit looking ridiculous in her massive coat of chain-mail, which covered her sloppily).

'We're in this together, right?' Manny reasoned. *Let's vote on it.*

They all looked at each other. Candlelight flickered. It did seem fair.

'Okay,' Manny said thirty seconds later, feeling deflated. 'Let's go outside.'

Chapter Twenty-six

The door swung violently open the second they turned the handle, and smashed against the stone balustrade that ran across the drawbridge. The water beneath might have been roused to coursing tidal waves by the wind for all they knew, but it was invisible, churning noisily in the dark shadows below.

Leaves and twigs were rushing through the air. The wind was actually shrieking in the trees.

Amina held her phone up, waving it over her head, and then kept looking at it. She jumped with excitement and went further outside. They all followed her, Cecil and Louis close by her side, all three supporting each other.

There was a large building by the edge of the gravel drive, which had perhaps been a stable or a barn. From Amina's gestures (it was impossible to hear her voice) as she neared it, she kept getting and losing the signal.

When the group gathered in the lee of the large wooden building, there was temporary respite. But they still couldn't hear each other talk. Elliott tried the handle of a rickety wooden door and they all yelped with delight when it opened.

'It's so frustrating,' said Amina. 'I just get it for a second, no more. It definitely gets better the more I move in this direction though ...' She waved her phone towards the mainland: south, away from the open sea and towards civilisation.

Then she looked round at the others, noticing that she'd received no reply. And saw that they were all looking at what was in the centre of the barn.

A gleaming purple four-wheel drive. With plump, healthy-looking tyres. Around the rest of the room were rusty toolboxes and shelves covered with gardening equipment.

'Oh wow,' she said. 'Are you thinking what I'm thinking?'

'I bloody hope not,' Manny admitted.

'If we can get this thing moving, we could drive until we get a full signal,' said Cecil. 'If we *can* ...'

After a pause, Elliott, who had been looking uncomfortable, straightened his back.

'Why are you all looking at me?' he said.

For a moment it was only the storm that spoke.

'Just because I'm from Hackney and a DJ,' he said. He opened his mouth to let out an aggrieved exclamation, and then suddenly something struck him as funny. He was genuinely tickled, and looked round at all of their faces. 'Okay, you think I'm some local gangsta. Yardie boy! I get it.' He was delighted. 'Ah, so the truth gets out. Um, yeah. I *used* to be a DJ. Ten years ago I was the best. But now? I couldn't get a gig if I tried. If I paid! I've done three gigs in the last few years: friends' weddings. In fact, I run a Bible study class at my local church ...'

'Wow,' said Manny.

'And the gym I run, that's technically part of the church too,' Elliott went on. 'It's the Gymnasium of the Friends of Jesus, on Borchello Road, kept alive by voluntary donation.'

'How bloody marvellous,' said Cecil.

'So you can't bust this car open then?' asked Fiona.

'I could get this thing moving,' said Louis. 'But it will involve damaging it. I'll have to break a window . . .'

Budget schmudget, thought Manny. *Insurance premiums schminsurance premiums.*

'There's no way you'll be able to reach the mainland,' said Manny. 'I can't believe it's me who's forced to be the voice of reason here – the least practical person on earth. But even I can see that's the point. *Stay on earth.* The road's probably got ten-foot waves crashing over it right now – you'll be drowned.'

'But it might also save our lives,' said Fiona.

Louis with his mighty strength made short work of the window, using a wrench wrapped in a cloth, and soon was in and working under the steering column with a pair of wire cutters.

The engine coughed, and then hummed. Louis turned and smiled modestly at the others, who looked at him with open admiration.

'Um, I can't actually drive,' he apologised.

'Well, I certainly bloody can't,' said Manny. 'Anyone else?' Amina, Cecil, Fiona shook their heads. Harry hesitated.

Louis stood back to make room for him to get in the front seat. The reaction was sudden and complete. He went white, and started to shake. 'I can't ... I can't ... Please don't make me ...'

'Sounds like you know how to, though,' said Cecil.

A sudden rush of wind hit the building. The barn felt like it rocked nearly off its foundations.

'You've been worrying if there's a killer among you,' said Harry, staring at the car, transfixed. 'And there is. It's me.'

'*Darling*,' said Manny. 'What are you ...'

'I was at a party with some mates,' said Harry in a hollow voice. 'We were all young lads. They wanted to drive home. But they were plastered. We'd have been ...' He swallowed. 'Well. I'd had a lot to drink, but it was just a lot less than they had. I insisted. And – we were turning a corner ...'

He'd gone deadly white. Fiona put an arm out to reassure him, but he shrugged it off, not wanting sympathy.

'We were turning a corner, and there was a woman walking her dog. What she was doing out at that time of night ...' He took a deep breath, looked up at the trembling rafters of the barn and seemed to make a resolution to get a hold of himself. 'I got ten years. I deserved it. That was 1979. I've spent the rest of my life trying to make up for it ...'

Manny was as stunned as anyone else. But she perceived that a light of sobriety had temporarily entered this madcap scheme. And she wanted to make the most of it, but couldn't quite think how. Short of begging.

'How horrible,' said Amina. She seemed to sum up the sentiment of the group. They wanted to give Harry sympathy, whether he deserved it or not. She hugged him, as he looked away, ashen faced.

'Fuck it, I'll give it a go,' said FlaymeZ.

'Yes, but *can you drive*?' Manny insisted.

'Of course,' she said, not meeting Manny's eye. 'I've played against my brother on *Gran Turismo*. Plenty.'

'Did you win?'

FlaymeZ examined the inside of the car, looked at the gear stick. Looked at Manny with an exasperated expression. 'He's my little brother. It's rude to win against a little 'un.'

'For god's sake, let's have a vote on it?' said Manny.

Police Interview Transcript

Interviewee: Manny Claudwinkle
Age: undetermined

Claudwinkle: What would you have done?

Inspector Constable: I'm the one asking the questions.

Claudwinkle: Okay, but just try to imagine for a second. What would you actually have done?

Inspector: I wouldn't have applied to go on a TV show about murdering.

Claudwinkle: Granted. But if, by hook or by crook, or some inconvenient coincidence, you found yourself there? Drive into a storm to save your lives, or stay in a castle where people are dying every half an hour?

Inspector: It's a difficult question to answer.

Claudwinkle: Thank you. So you concede I was not in the easiest situation on this earth.

Inspector: Let's press on with the questions. So you voted on it . . .

Chapter Twenty-seven

Manny looked out from the first-floor window at the front of the castle.

'I hope those guys are okay,' she said.

'God bless them,' said Amina, looking over her shoulder.

'They're mad,' said Cecil. 'But – yes. God bless them.'

Those who were to remain in the castle had all gone back inside, across the drawbridge, and barricaded the front door with great difficulty, as the wind was flapping it violently back and forth.

The others – Louis, FlaymeZ, Harry and Elliott – were in the car and ready to go. They'd waited until the main group were safely back inside, and signalling to them from the first-floor window, before setting off. Both groups were waving to each other.

The car backed hesitantly out of the barn, in a hiccuppy, stop-start fashion, knocking over a tall pile of flowerpots and then turning the other way and dismembering some wooden shelves, which made a pallet of clay tiles spill across the car roof.

Manny thought about her teenage son, the games he was always playing in the living room. Was *Gran Turismo* one of those? She was pretty sure it was. You played that with a PlayStation controller, not even a steering wheel!

'Oh god,' she said. 'Oh god, oh god.'

There seemed to be some commotion within the car as it reversed onto the gravel drive. Manny could only imagine how the loud arguments and conflicting advice within would add to the quality of the driving.

Pointing the car towards the road leading out of the estate, FlaymeZ put her foot down and the wheels spun madly.

At once the car shot backwards towards the castle.

'She hasn't changed gear,' said Cecil.

'My god, they've smashed through the stone pillars!' said Amina.

Manny said nothing. She couldn't speak. The car had vanished into the moat. A perfunctory splash rose up, a spray that was whipped away in the wind.

Then, worse, the castle insiders watched as a section of stone balustrade, knocked loose by the passage of the car, tilted and then plunged downwards, coming to rest visibly on the car's roof.

There was panic.

They wanted to help. But they had tied the castle door closed with a length of rope tied in twelve thick knots. They wanted to rush and find another exit from the castle, presuming there was one that would let them out. So they could get to the moat and . . .

What? Dive down into it? Let each other down with ropes? And suppose someone had survived? Attach them to ropes somehow and lift them up by physical force . . . while simultaneously treading water, in a storm?

It was obviously impossible. Instead they shouted, pointed, made ridiculous suggestions.

They were paralysed with helplessness.

But no one left the car. It was a dark, malevolent shadow which, once still, transmitted to the onlookers nothing except fear.

They had all grown quiet again, and were looking through the window, their hearts leaping out of their chests.

'"Only one of you will survive",' said Amina, who was the first to tear her eyes away. She looked at the others.

'And then there were four,' said Cecil.

'To use a Glaswegian expression,' said Fiona, '*fuck.*'

Chapter Twenty-eight

They were down to the final handful of logs in the basket beside the fire. The Mead Hall was big enough to take them all with space to spare, and give them room enough to stay far away from one another.

The superb acoustics allowed them to hear each other clearly. Even over the booming outside.

'Think about it,' said Fiona. 'The killer must be in this room.'

'But I trust you all ...' said Amina. 'One hundred per cent. I mean – I want to. I really instinctively think that you are all ... I mean, I literally can't believe you'd be involved in something like this.'

'There is no "this". It was an accident,' said Manny. 'We all saw that.'

'But you could have put the idea in their heads, Amina,' said Cecil, dismally unhappy in the firelight. 'Or you, Fiona. And cut the brakes. Or anyone could have.'

'So we're agreed they were all Faithfuls?' said Fiona.

'Poor Louis,' said Cecil. 'He was a tortured soul. I saw him – more than once – taking bottles of wine into his room. I'm convinced that's what he was doing earlier, when he said he slipped off to the loo. It's why people started suspecting him, which is why I think he decided to leave in the car ...'

'I never heard him slur his words,' said Amina. 'But one night I did catch him topping up one of the wine bottles with water. We both pretended it was all a hilarious joke, and we giggled while he put it up on the shelf where no one would find it for ages. But it did worry me.'

'My god,' said Manny.

'But you don't necessarily smell of booze when you're an alcoholic,' said Fiona. 'I mean, if you're not homeless that is. Trust me, I'm a Glaswegian. You southerners think you can drink, but with us lot it's vodka rather than mother's milk. I saw him doing stuff too. I wasn't going to say so. But I've long known the signs and I saw them in him.'

'Poor *bastard*,' said Manny.

She was horrified. A whole part of the production process was getting to know the candidates – contestants – whatever you wanted to call them. It might be cringeworthy to say so out loud, but by the end of the process Manny genuinely thought of them all as friends.

She talked to the contestants individually for many hours during the preparation for the series. This was vetting, of course – but it was essential emotional prep. To build friendliness and trust. She genuinely got to know them.

Or she thought she did.

Only one of you will survive, she thought, picturing that assured handwriting in ink on vintage paper. Such care taken to make it and to place it where they would find it.

She shuddered.

Little Louis – who managed to shrink his hulking six-foot-four frame into a humble, softly spoken person you hardly noticed. Louis the sensitive reader of Italian poetry and Japanese literature, as well as a muscular mechanic who could flip a metal motorbike chassis over without effort (as he did in the video inserts of him they'd already recorded, for later broadcast), and who was literally the only gay in his Cornish village.

To find out he was so severe an alcoholic that he was stealing bottles of wine from the set of the show . . .

'All of them in the car were innocent,' said Fiona. 'Even if they didn't think they were in some ways,' she added, thinking of Harry.

'Because they wanted to leave?' Manny asked.

'Because they were killed,' said Fiona.

Cecil agreed.

'If it was tampered with,' said Manny. 'I just please want you all to consider that it might be an accident. Just a series of accidents. One terrible accident naturally makes people act erratically and makes another more likely. Don't you see that's what's happened?'

'I think so,' said Cecil guardedly.

'I'm pretty sure I listened to a podcast that said something similar,' said Amina. 'I *think* I did.'

'But what Manny's saying is something the killer might say, to make us lower our defences,' said Fiona.

'Okay, I know we're all in a heightened state of paranoia, but just remember what I said *might also be true* . . .'

'What about what was written on that note?' Fiona asked. '"All of us are guilty"? Well, *I've* not hurt anybody.'

'Maybe you wrote it then,' said Amina. 'I don't know what I'm guilty of. I'm . . .'

Amina was wielding a medieval crossbow. Which one might not have thought was a very dangerous proposition after sitting around on a shelf for four hundred years, except that beside it in its glass case had been a note saying: 'Medieval crossbow – remodelled and fully functional.'

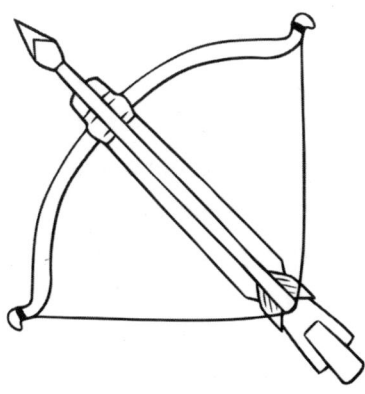

She was visibly growing tired. She swung the crossbow from corner to corner, as though to check neither of the other survivors had advanced a pace or two, with malicious intent.

'You can trust me, Amina,' said Cecil. He spoke gently, warmheartedly.

She swung the crossbow towards him.

'Not you!' she said. 'It's you I'm most afraid of. People like you . . .' The weight of holding the crossbow up suddenly told on her arms. She leant against the wall and slid to the ground, where she sat with it propped on her knees. That was easier.

'I don't think you know what you mean when you say,

"people like you",' said Cecil in the same understand-
ing tone.

'My name's not Amina,' she said. In her new position
she was able to fix him much more accurately in her
sights.

'What is it then, hun?' Manny asked. She felt the ground
shifting under her feet.

'It's Hannah,' said Amina. 'Which is a traditional Syrian
name. I chose Amina because it sounds more – ironically,
I guess – *authentic* to British ears.'

'Why?' asked Fiona.

'What do you mean?' asked Manny.

'I'm an immigrant,' said Hannah.

'So?' Fiona and Manny said together.

'An *illegal* immigrant,' Hannah said. 'I came over on a
boat. Like the sort that you and your party hate. And think
are ruining the country, Cecil . . .'

Cecil's eyes were round. 'That's not how I feel, my
friend . . .' he said softly.

'Ours was one of the boats that wasn't caught,' Hannah
said. 'And I had a cousin to meet me, and he hid me, and
got me work, and slowly – by working hard – I managed
to get my own place and build a life. A lie! But a life. God,
I was lucky! Until today, that is . . .'

'Why'd you apply to come on the show then, darling?'
asked Manny in her kindest voice.

Hannah shrank into herself. 'I've worked so hard for
what I've got – my job and my house. But I, maybe it's
understandable given my history, but I struggle to trust
people and make friends. To be . . . faithful, I suppose. I
don't knit, I don't play sport. I joined a choir but I can't

136

sing. It was just a long shot, to do something out of the ordinary. I never thought I'd get on ...'

'I admire you so much,' Cecil said. He looked like he wanted to give her a hug.

'Don't come a step closer,' she said. 'Not one step. My life is good. At last. At least it was until tonight. The identity I made was bulletproof − it would never have been discovered ...'

'For my part,' Cecil said, 'there's a lot of complexity you don't understand. I was a Labour councillor. Then I turned Tory. I saw what people needed. I knew their problems. And I saw how badly served they were by their councillors. I was determined to help. There was one project that was going to cost thousands of jobs − a bypass that would ruin our town. Ruin businesses, lives, communities. No one was trying to stop it except me.'

'Then you turned *Reform UK*?' Fiona asked. 'What the fuck?'

'I knew that there were lots of disappointed Labour voters who would go for it. I just did what I had to do to stay in, to enact the policies I believed in. Which were certainly *not* those of the wider party. And it worked − I got it stopped. I promise you I was the only person committed to this issue. And I swayed with the prevailing wind, for the best chance of looking after the people I love.'

He stopped and looked at them, as well as he could in the flickering firelight. There was a sense of scepticism in the room.

'As it happens, there's no immigration issue where I'm from. It's not something voters care about. And even if they did ... I didn't campaign on that issue. I truly think the people who voted for me were good people. I care about people, not where they are from.'

They all thought about this. Cecil, who was closest to the fire, went and added another log to it. Only a few left. Smoke billowed down the chimney as it was pounded from above by the storm winds.

'Well,' said Fiona, 'I don't think you know the truth about me. I kept it secret from your producers.'

'You're gay,' said Manny, realising as she said it how stupid a comment it was.

Fiona laughed. 'Obviously I'm gay. Look at me. By the way, have you ever seen Glaswegian men? They'd turn anyone into a dyke. No ...' She adjusted the musket she was holding in the crook of her arm to make it more comfortable. 'Um, I'm actually going to inherit this castle.'

'What!' said Manny.

Hannah laughed. 'You're bloody kidding me!'

'When I'm kidding you, you'll soon know about it,' said Fiona flatly. 'When my aunt dies, and she's not looking too healthy at the moment (but then who am I to talk), this whole place comes to me. And I've got bad news for ya – this castle is fucked. It needs two million quid's worth of repairs to even be put on the market. It looks fine from the outside, sure, but the innards are buggered.'

'Wait ...' said Manny. She looked again at the folder of unread (and to her, it would seem, for some reason unreadable) messages Damian Shraw had given her earlier in the day. It was on the floor in front of her.

I slightly wish I'd listened to him now, she thought.

'When this series stops airing, as a family we'll have no income,' said Fiona. 'And it costs fifty grand a year to keep this place as it is. Nah, it's fucked. No rooms upstairs to rent out. No electricity, no running water (don't know if you've noticed). The National Trust can't afford to do the place up. It will fall back into ruin. I decided to try to come on the show as a last-ditch attempt to get some of the money it will take to repair it.'

'You must have felt so proud that the castle was used in the show though,' said Hannah.

Fiona curled her lip and looked up at the gothic hammerbeam roof.

'Not really. Don't like telly much meself. Prefer the bingo,' she said, sniffing. 'Nah, this shithole will fall back off the map and what the family gets for the land will cover our debts from keeping it, with ten shillings to spare ...'

She sighed, and in the gloom, to Manny's watching eyes, appeared momentarily to fume like a dragon, a plume rising about her head and her eyes gleaming.

Hannah yelped, and Manny was about to do the same, then Fiona removed the vape from her mouth. Those weren't allowed on the island either.

'Smuggled it in in me sock,' she said to Manny, and winked.

'Cripes,' said Cecil. Then he seemed to rethink this expression. 'I mean, shit,' he added.

'Jeez,' said Manny.

'That's mad, Fiona,' said Hannah. 'How about you, Manny?'

'Hmm? What?' She'd been lost in thought. They were all looking at her.

'This might be the last night of our lives,' said Cecil.

'What else have we got to do except tell tales around the fireside? What's your secret?'

'Tell tales? You want me to tell you the secrets of the other players?' she asked. Since all bets were off, she started to say, 'Well, you know who's actually a recovered—' but Hannah cut her off.

'No. *Your* secrets.'

'You must have some,' said Cecil.

Just because all you freaks seem to? she wanted to ask.

'You're a TV person, after all,' said Fiona. 'We know what you lot get up to. Is it true that before going on telly Terry Wogan used to nervously knead a bucket full of . . .'

Manny shook her head. Firelight glinted off her eyes.

'No,' she said. 'No, no, no. No secrets. Me? No. Not a secret to be found.' She looked into the flames. 'Not one!' she said.

Chapter Twenty-nine

'I gave you a chance when I offered you this job,' said Jed Burkitt viciously. 'Now repay that trust and get me an effing star guest for tomorrow's programme or we're going *off the air*! Then we'll all be out of a job!'

He'd given this speech, or one very like it, five times already to the other members of the team over the last few days. Which, seeing as the office was a small one, meant this was the sixth time she'd received the verbal assault. Albeit the first time directly to her face.

The other production staff were a hardened bunch: cynical, ambitious, impervious to criticism. Faith wished she could be that way.

'I'll do it,' she promised. She sweated profusely when stressed, and even more so in this stuffy office when the pressure was on. It made her wild, frizzy blonde hair even more unmanageable.

Jed stalked back into his office and slammed the door, which made the cheap plastic venetian blind jump and jiggle nervously, and then settle in an ungainly posture half askew. In a fury, he ripped it off and threw it at the bin.

If I lose this job, that's me done in London, thought Faith. *Back to bloody Sussex. Working in that goddamned primary school with my mum and my sister and that witch Mrs Avery who used to spank me.*

I would actually rather be dead, she thought.

The show they were all working on, from their un-air-conditioned fifth-floor Wardour Street office, was *Lunchtime*. It was not brilliant. But there wasn't much competition on the other three channels at that time of day. It didn't take much to get a decent audience share.

Half the population, the intelligent half, was in the grip of the Barcelona Olympics, and wearily grinding itself up towards a general election later in the year, when they would find out whether the wimpish head prefect John Major could somehow keep the Conservatives in power for a few more years. It looked bloody unlikely.

The other half of the population were the people who watched *Lunchtime*.

These were the hideous dog days of August, when nothing happened and all the useful people were on holiday.

Faith was not an aggressive go-getter like the other cocaine-fuelled gits in the office. She wished she had their confidence. Unless it turned her into them, of course, in which case she didn't want it. But she didn't think it would. She thought she could put confidence to a more profitable use. She knew she was clever, and she was sincerely *dying* to work in telly. She *literally loved it* so much.

Lunchtime had been on air for sixteen weeks, of this series at least. Which was its fifteenth series. Perhaps understandably at this point, the guests were running dry. (Mainly because everyone useful was on holiday.) The immediate reason for panic was that word had come down that the head of the channel was coming to watch tomorrow's show. And the option for renewal was up next week.

What's more, the ratings (although who knew how they were calculated? By phone poll?) were said to be down.

That was ominous. Somehow they had to pull the best show they'd ever done out of the bag, or they were all fired.

Faith had only a few ideas left. And not much hope in any of them.

There was a snake charmer who had famously nearly been throttled by one of his own animals, on camera. She'd met him in a Camden bar. He seemed interested, but he hadn't really looked at her face. His eyes had not raised above the level of the centre of her chest, which seemed to give the lie to his averred interest in the show.

More snake than charmer, she had decided.

There was the astrologer to Princess Diana, who had agreed to come on the show, then decided it wasn't in their stars and cancelled.

Then there was an opera singer, whose manager she'd met. They were very keen to get him on television to promote a new tour he was starting. But Faith had it on good authority that he knew literally not a single word of English. And the show didn't really have money for a translator. But then even if they did – surely a translated conversation would make for deathly television?

Faith racked her brains. Think. Think! Everything rests on this moment. If only I had the confidence, the stage presence, of . . .

She was not a regular in the comedy clubs. But a friend had brought her along a few nights earlier to a place in

Soho where a character act had brought the house down. Faith, sat in the front row, hadn't laughed once. Because she'd had her mouth open in awe the whole time.

The act was so funny, so quick, so charming. So brilliant and fearless. She didn't even have a routine that she trotted out – it was all crowd work. Clever, silly, a bit rude – and *not* mean. But so funny.

I need to channel Manny Claudwinkle, Faith thought.

And then: *We need Manny on the show!*

Chapter Thirty

'Yeah?' said a gravelly voice through the intercom.
'It's Faith Meadows,' said Faith. 'Can I—'

'Fuck off,' said the voice, followed by a few other choice phrases, and a click.

Faith looked at the piece of paper in her hand again, and cinching her bag further up her shoulder, tried another bell.

'What?' said a voice.

'I was hoping to talk to Jill Smith,' she said.

'She's not here.'

'That's the right number then? I'm sorry, I wrote it down all squiggly. I've spoken to about three of your neighbours. Cheerful lot,' she said.

There was no response.

'We spoke on the phone,' said Faith. 'I'm from the television production company.'

'Oh, thank Christ,' said the voice. 'I thought you were from the debt collectors. They're always trying to find me.'

There was a buzz.

*

'You *won't?*' said Faith. She was standing next to a woman her own height and her own weight, with short-cropped black hair. They were both looking at a settee where Manny's costume was laid out: long straight brown wig, shiny top, skinny trousers, pointy heels. Bangles, neck-laces, earrings. The effect was as though she had been zapped into space by aliens who, presumably, wanted to meet someone exquisite and with a lot of dazzle. Albeit the zapper had transported her fully nude, leaving her earthly accoutrements behind.

'That gig you came to see the other night,' said Jill, 'it was great. But it was my last. I can't afford to keep doing this character. I liked it when I first moved to London, but I've been offered a promotion in my job and I can't afford not to take it. I was performing for five quid a time, and it knocks me out the next day and is affecting my work.'

'What do you during the day?' Faith asked.

'Political lobbyist. It's not the best, but it's a good job. There are opportunities, and I can pay the rent. All I need is for one of my bosses to get wind of all this stage stuff, and that's it. Fired. Back to my gran's bakery in Bucks, serving bacon baps to perverts.' Jill shuddered with hatred.

Faith nodded sadly. She felt a true sense of kinship, and wanted to put a hand out to reassure Jill she felt the same way, but she wasn't even confident enough to do that.

Faith hadn't really understood what she'd been looking at during the comedy night. A character act, she'd thought, was perhaps the real person with a dab more make-up or something. But now she'd met Jill, she saw it was a persona, an alter ego, one that gave Jill power she didn't feel when alone in this (frankly unpleasant) sixteenth-floor flat.

'I won't say it's not been fun,' said Jill. 'It has. But the only people who persevere in this business are geniuses, or deranged, or lucky. Some all three. But mostly the latter two.'

'Just one appearance. On telly. Tomorrow,' said Faith. She was promising, although she wasn't at all sure that her boss would book her, when she brought this idea to him.

Jill shook her head firmly. It was obviously difficult for her. After all the effort she had put in to the character, here was the opportunity she'd hoped for all those years, while struggling as a performer on stage.

She absent-mindedly stroked a mole at the corner of her eye which, in public, she normally kept covered in make-up. Wondering, perhaps, whether this glittering sight on the horizon, this prospect Faith was offering up, was in fact the longed-for oasis, or just another mirage. But no – her mind was made up.

'Not interested. The character's dead.'

Faith felt a wellspring of tragedy so sincere that she put her hand to her chest. Tears trembled silently in the corners of her eyes.

'I just thought she was *so beautiful*,' Faith said. 'She gave me courage.'

Jill walked over and picked up the wig. 'She still can,' she said, tossing it to her.

Chapter Thirty-one

In an alleyway beside the TV studio, which was filled with giant metal bins and wet rubbish, a door popped open and someone came out.

She was tottering on five-inch heels, and she clutched the handrail as she went down the metal stairs. She was breathing hard. Deep, long breaths, let out slow.

She fished her keys out of a pocket, then dropped them. Stooped and picked them up, then went to the side of a rusty Honda Civic and unlocked it. Got in, and sat for a moment in the front seat.

Breathe in, breathe out. She patted the steering wheel with her hands. Then again, harder. With more emotion. One hand accidentally pressed the horn which honked briefly. She looked around, waiting for someone to appear and tell her off. When they didn't, she laughed.

'That was amazing,' she said. 'That was amazing. You're amazing, Manny. I love you.' And pulling her wig off, she started to shake out her frizzy blonde hair.

She hit the horn again, hard this time.

At the top of the stairs the door popped open and a stage manager stuck his head out.

'Oi, love!' he shouted. 'You want to do me a favour and shut up making that fucking noise?' Then he disappeared inside again.

In the car, she laughed throatily. Not Faith's nervous giggle. Manny's laugh.

Chapter Thirty-two

'Where did you find her?' asked Jed, leering at her over the desk.

Faith had never until this moment had a backbone, that she had been able to locate. She knew other people had them, and dinosaurs too – she'd seen them in museums. Great thirty-foot-long spines, with fifty or so vertebrae like piano stools held together apparently with Play-Doh. But up until now, to her, spines had been something exotic that only other creatures had.

'I can't tell you,' she said, feeling a zing of strength down her back. She literally could not tell him. For his own good.

He looked at her uncertainly. For a moment it was like he was going to explode with bad temper. Then, bemused, he decided to find it funny.

'Well, the channel head thought she was hilarious. The studio audience thought she was hilarious too. Which was more than half the battle. I think he's convinced this show is better than he'd thought it was. We'll have her back. And soon.'

He meant this not as an observation but as a direct and immediate order.

'Where are Charles and Adrian?' asked Faith, looking at two nearby empty desks, and surprising herself by her own boldness.

'They're gone,' Jed said dismissively. 'Charles was on drugs. Stupid bugger. And Adrian was selling him the drugs. Bloody idiot. But more than that, they were useless. Listen, tell me when that Manny character's going to appear next, on stage. I'd like to see her.'

Faith nodded. Her hand was clutching the wig which was on her lap, under the desk. 'I'll ask her. I know she's pretty booked up, but I'll try . . .'

'You'd better. Don't let her get away. She's a shot in the arm for this show.'

He closed the door to his office and (visible through the gap where he'd torn down the blind) flopped into the chair at his desk. Faith waited until he'd picked up the phone and started a conversation with someone else before she let her breath out.

She looked down at the desk in front of her. There were three handwritten messages, all of them asking to be put in touch with Manny. All of them apparently offers of work.

She quietly got on with her day. On the outside she was pretty certain she looked utterly normal and unchanged. But something had altered inside Faith Meadows.

She knew she'd found something she wanted to do for the rest of her life. Someone she wanted to be. In fact, if all went to plan, she might not be Faith Meadows that much longer.

Her pulse jabbed at an excited rate.

The future suddenly looked . . .

'I can't believe you've done this,' someone said.

'We trusted you.'

Faith looked around the office. Fear and confusion rose in her.

'You've betrayed us . . .'

Chapter Thirty-three

S he started awake.

'We *trusted* you,' Fiona was saying.

'You betrayed us ...' Hannah was distraught, wiping a tear from her cheek.

Manny looked around wildly. Remembered the storm. The awful deaths. The fact that she was in imminent danger.

How the hell had she managed to fall asleep?

'What are you talking about, my darlings?' she said sleepily. 'I haven't betrayed anyone.'

'You said you had no secrets.'

'I *have* no secrets,' she said doggedly, shaking off the memory of the dream she'd just woken from.

Cecil laughed hollowly.

The three of them were standing at the Dodecahedral Table in the centre of the room. They were leafing through some papers, holding them up to the light. Manny saw that they were the contents of the folder she'd been told (again and again (and again)) and that she had promised

(repeatedly and with apparent sincerity (again and again))
to read.

She got tiredly to her feet and came over.

'Stay back!' shouted Cecil. He was wielding a sword.

'What's in there?' Manny asked. 'I've been meaning to get round to . . . I've not read those . . .'

'Nice try,' said Hannah, bitterly. 'This is beyond anything I might have expected. I knew you'd do background checks on us, but this . . .'

'You've got dirt on us all,' said Cecil, astounded. 'Stuff even we didn't know about.'

'What do you mean?' Manny asked. What could they possibly have found in there? The production had scrounged up their tax returns or something? What the hell was this?

Cecil flicked through some pages. 'Look at this. Enwyn helped to expose the corruption of one of his neighbours. The famous case of the hundred-year-old major who raised money during Covid, and the daughter who was accused of helping that money disappear. Well – look here. The daughter killed herself while under investigation and it turns out it wasn't her who was taking the money after all, but her accountant . . .'

'And Elliott,' said Fiona, 'he was a bastion of his local community, a helper of troubled youths, a member of his church. But he sponsored a woman who was just out of prison and then started having an affair with her, and when she started stealing money from him, he lied to her probation officer and said she wasn't doing it.'

'FlaymeZ retweeted a song to her hundred-thousand followers mocking a priest who'd been caught lying. A video of the priest being caught out was doing the rounds that night. He then had a breakdown and the charity he ran lost all its funding in twenty-four hours, and closed, leaving thousands of people without the support they needed. It later turned out the "gotcha" video was just a misunderstanding . . .'

Hannah looked up from what she was reading to Manny. 'There's nothing about me here. Or Louis. There are probably some pages missing . . .'

'You amassed folders on us all,' said Cecil. 'So you could control us. I expect you only brought people onto the show who you could blackmail if it came to it. If you needed to for some reason.'

'She could be the killer,' said Fiona. 'This is her motivation. Avenging all these wrongs.'

'*Stop* it,' said Manny. 'I didn't know what was in there. I knew the production team did background checks, of course I did, but . . .' She wondered for a second if some of their accusations could be true. Was Damian a criminal mastermind after all? Oh *surely* not, not hand-sanitiser guy . . .

'They hire a firm of detectives to check up on you,' she stammered. 'I'm only dimly aware of it . . .'

'Only dimly?' yelled Cecil, furiously holding up a sheet of paper. 'This was in an email to you!'

Manny had that dizzying and sickening realisation that a full (and absolutely factual) explanation right at this moment could not sound like anything other than desperate and made up. ('I'm awful at reading my emails and so they were printed and handed to me just today by coincidence . . .' etc., etc.) She could do nothing except plough on.

155

'I think we've changed the firm we use recently and these new guys have just been overzealous.'

They kept reading, handing sheets to each other.

'I didn't know about this – or, if I had, I would have stopped it,' she blathered. 'I don't think they were ever going to use this stuff in any way – it's just automatic to do background checks when so much rides on your participation . . . Millions of pounds . . .'

They weren't listening.

She tried to explain that she'd only been a producer for a few weeks and hadn't really caught up with her new responsibilities yet. That she'd only taken on the role in extreme reluctance, to keep the programme alive. To (therefore, by extension) keep their dreams alive . . . And she never had time to . . . Perhaps she ought to have paid her children to read them onto voice notes (no, god, don't say that – an even more flagrant breach of trust) . . .

She floundered and saw she was losing their trust once and for all. No matter what she said. And just because of those god-flipping-damned papers she'd held under her arm all afternoon and all night! (If they kept reading, what other blinking mother-loving heck would they find in there?) She kept talking, but heard a pleading note entering her own voice.

Somehow it can be impossible to seem credible to an audience who are convinced you're guilty. Perversely, the more you try to appear innocent, the guiltier you come across.

'Don't you see, Manny,' said Cecil, 'this information could have got into the wrong hands? Anyone with an exaggerated sense of injustice, and suffering from paranoia.

A person under a lot of pressure, perhaps – for instance, someone appearing on a reality TV show where they think they're about to be murdered at any time. They could read these things and decide we were all evil and beneath contempt . . .'

'Worth killing,' said Fiona.

Manny could see that that was . . . *possible*. Distantly.

Possible, but also ridiculous. She wasn't the most security-conscious of individuals. Really, anyone could have taken the pages from her at any time. But that was irrelevant – any killer would have needed these things months, *months* ago. And – sure! – her computer passwords were quite possibly not the safest. But . . . this meant someone having access to her home device.

Someone who knew her already before this series (not season) started! And who had a talent for murdering people while making the killings appear like accidental deaths! Boring, nervous Damian Shraw? Handsome and capable (but dead) Yukio? Wonderfully named and titled (but god bless her, not that bright) Head of Beauty Solaris Benedicta?

As all these sarcastic rationalisations of their accusations flooded her brain, her apparent hesitation told the Faithfuls that they already had everything they needed to know.

'These murders are your fault, Manny!' Fiona said.

'But look at you all,' she said. 'You're scared out of your skins. If these ghastly deaths *are* murders, who actually *did* them?'

Lightning struck a tree outside and all the windows flashed simultaneously.

And there came a heavy knock on the hall door. Everyone screamed.

Chapter Thirty-four

Cecil, Hannah and Fiona grabbed each other for support. There was a clattering as all the weapons they had been clutching fell to the floor. And then a frantic scurry as they got down and searched around on all fours to try and pick them up again.

Fiona picked up her bow and arrow, Hannah her crossbow and Cecil, unable to locate the rapier he'd been holding, rushed to the wall and climbed up on a chair to pull down a mighty battle-axe that was hanging there.

Manny wouldn't know what to do with a weapon if she had one. So she was glad she didn't. But there was a length of lead pipe nearby she was eyeing up if anyone came too close with the wrong idea.

The knocking came a second time. Three heavy blows. Slow and dismal, like the knocks of death itself.

'Who's there?' shouted Fiona.

'Don't come in!' yelled Hannah. 'We're armed!'

The handle started to turn, slowly, until it had gone through ninety degrees. The door didn't open. There was a pause, during which the thunder following on behind the lightning that had just flashed resounded mightily around the roof.

Then the door opened.

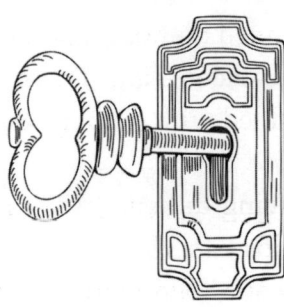

A tall figure stood there, wrapped in a cloak. One of the Secret Murderers' cloaks. Face obscured. They all screamed again. It really did seem the thing to do.

Fiona loosed her arrow, which flew with shocking speed right into the centre of the figure. Hannah fired her bolt simultaneously. The figure staggered in place then stumbled stupidly. Fell onto its knees.

The cloak hood slid back.

Hannah screamed. A scream of terror and woe, right up at the ceiling,

'My god,' said Fiona quietly.

'It's Yukio the cameraman!' said Manny. 'He was alive all this time! You murdering bastards!'

'I thought you took his pulse?' said Cecil from the other side of the room.

'Oh, eff you,' Manny said. 'I took it ten times!'

Yukio slumped forward. As he slammed into the ground, the arrow in his chest was forced through. Face down on the floor, the cloak was tented where the arrow extended through his back.

Even from where she was crouched, Manny could see the hideous jutting aberration in Yukio's neck. It was so pronounced it threw a shadow in the firelight. He must have lain there stunned for hours and then, coming round, stumbled in here bewildered and terrified, looking for help.

The room was filled with firelight and desperation, and not much faith.

Hannah was having difficulty with her crossbow, desperately trying to load another bolt.

'I've killed someone,' said Fiona quietly.

Cecil, who had missed all the action, had finally got the enormous battle-axe off the wall. But it was so top-heavy he was having difficulty carrying it.

Then everything happened at once. In the difficult light, Cecil failed to see the covered-up form of Enwyn on the floor. He tripped, and trying to keep hold of the battle-axe, went running forward at a desperate uncontrolled canter, as the blade swung down.

With great effort, Hannah managed to get a second bolt into the crossbow. She had been bent over it, straining with both hands. As she straightened, she saw the uncontrolled blade of the battle-axe falling directly towards her face. It landed on the crown of her head, bisecting it down to the bridge of her nose.

The crossbow bolt she'd just loaded, fired.

It hit Fiona in the centre of the chest. She sat heavily on the floor, then rolled sideways.

Cecil gasped, looking from one to the other. Hannah fell away backwards, obviously and totally dead. Fiona lay with blinking eyes, apparently trying to speak. Cecil went over to her and gathered her in his arms.

'I'm so sorry.'

'I love you, Cecil,' said Fiona. 'Even if you are a posh fucker.' She smiled weakly. 'Sorry for ruining your nice jacket. By the way. I was a Faithful. One hundred per cent.'

'I'm one of the Murderers!' wailed Cecil. 'I confess! I'm a Murderer!'

'He means in the game!' said Manny desperately, suddenly seeing what was about to happen and trying to prevent it. Fiona, in her dying confusion, had got the wrong end of the stick. She thought he was telling the literal truth, and she was lying in the lap of a killer.

On the floor by her hand was a dagger, discarded by one of the other players. With her last gasp of strength she took it up and stuck it in Cecil's side, up to the hilt.

He died instantly.

Chapter Thirty-five

'Guys?' said Manny.

The only reply she got was from the wind, its shriek sharpening.

'Guys?' Manny insisted. 'No way. No way are you all . . .'

She got up and stepped forward cautiously. There was no human sound in the room at all except for her own breathing.

'This can't be happening,' she said. 'It's a joke, right? Guys?' she added. She really did not like being alone. It was kind of selfish of them all to have left her like this.

What time was it?

God knew. Small hours maybe.

She went to the Dodecahedral Table and, getting on her hands and knees, crawled underneath it. It was the only place where she could feel safe. *Let's just stay here until someone comes,* she thought. *Let's just stay here if someone doesn't ever come. Let's just stay here. Nice table. Safe table.*

Might be hours, might be days. Just stay here and don't do anything, and don't even think.

Her knee knocked against something as she crawled. It

was a pile of shallow boxes that rattled as they fell over. There was just about enough light from the fire at this angle for her to make some things out. Having something to look at and pay attention to was good.

She picked up one of the boxes and shook it. Little things chockled about in its insides. She looked at the cover until she could make it out. *Trivial Pursuit.*

Ah, she thought. Must tell Keith I've found it.

She picked up another.

This cover was darker and she had to strain to read it. But slowly her eyes adjusted. She made out the words on the back.

'"All of you are guilty",' she read aloud. '"Only one of you will survive."'

She stared at it stupidly for a long time. She listened to the spindly crackle of the fire and the depressed, insistent groaning of the wind outside. She knew those words but they failed to penetrate. There was a flicker of light through the windows again and a while later another distant rumble.

She mouthed the words. Still didn't understand them.

She turned the box round. *Murder at Grimstone Castle* was the name of the game, she saw at last. The back cover was easier to read. 'Can you guess who the killer is before the end?' asked the text at the bottom. 'Can *you* be the last one to survive?'

She lifted the lid off the box and chucked it away impatiently. Inside was a board, a pad of character sheets and several decks of cards. A little baggy filled with movable pieces, still unopened. In one corner of the set was a rectangular space where some part of the game was missing.

Fishing in her pocket, she brought out the envelope they'd found in the library.

It fit in the rectangular space perfectly.

She nodded.

Now it all made sense.

Chapter Thirty-six

'M ade sense?' Inspector Constable asked.
'Well, yes,' Manny said tiredly.

'Can you explain it to me?' he asked.

'Someone had been playing with the game, and the envelope had got free from the box. They'd accidentally left it in the library, where we found it. And it freaked everyone out.'

'I'm not sure that explains everything,' said the inspector.

'I don't know if I *can* explain everything,' said Manny. 'But I've told you everything I know. Everything I saw. I've told you everything.'

'But the card, did that explain ...?' said Inspector Constable.

'They all claimed to trust each other, to be faithful,' she said. 'And they believed that they all were (except for the Secret Murderers, obviously). But when we found that card they started getting seriously paranoid, thinking there was no such thing as a Faithful. They found out what the game would be like *played for real*. And, in consequence, made increasingly terrible decisions. I tried to stop them at every turn. To dilute their paranoia. I wanted to protect them. But thanks to that one random coincidence, I couldn't control their fears.'

'And this folder of papers from the producer,' the inspector said. 'This contains the information that had been ferreted out about these people. This unnecessarily scurrilous detail, that scared them so badly.'

'Yes,' Manny said, clutching her forehead. 'It's mad. It was a powder keg. Why had anyone written this stuff down, let alone printed it out and handed it to me?'

'It was just bad luck they all had skeletons in the closet?' the detective asked.

'I guess so?' Manny asked in return. 'But maybe anyone might have, if people look hard enough. Harry had been rude to someone in a bakery in Devon. They'd refused to serve him – he'd accused them publicly of doing so because he was gay. It was a cause célèbre. The bakery, which had been in the family since 1876, had to close, went out of business. In fact, the owner was herself gay, but didn't want to come out while her parents were still alive. So she couldn't defend herself. She developed a drinking problem. All the family are now dead.'

'A sad story,' said Constable. 'So – he was a hypocrite.'

Manny snorted. 'Can you prove he really did wrong? It's a matter of perspective, surely . . .'

'Look,' she went on. 'Judith had arrested a teacher in front of his entire school for crimes that turned out to be perpetrated by someone else. He never worked again, the school lost several staff members who resigned in protest, it dropped fifty places in the performance tables and never recovered. Even in the face of these events, she publicly claimed afterwards to have done nothing wrong. The report showed her in a bad light. Did it prove she'd knowingly done evil?'

'But wait a minute,' said Constable. 'The cameraman. He was a snooper – a pervert?'

Manny shook her head. 'Speak to Shraw. That was in the papers too. Obsessive-compulsive health boy Damian was afraid we had an infestation of rodents. People had seen droppings. It would be a health and safety infraction that would potentially shut us down while we got exterminators in from the city, fifty miles away. We weren't actually using those bathroom facilities while he was investigating.'

'I see you read the papers at last.'

'There was nothing else to do, waiting for you lot to turn up,' said Manny. 'And after I'd read the instruction leaflets for all the games.'

'How are you going to prove that all this happened the way you said it did?' asked the inspector, sitting back in his chair.

She stared at him with empty eyes. After a pause, she shook her head wearily and shrugged.

'Well, lucky for you,' Constable said, 'it turns out that the cameras were still working all that time. They have their own independent batteries and back-up storage units. They work for up to twelve hours without mains electricity. We've looked at the footage.'

Manny was awake again, and alert. She pointed a finger at him. 'Right!' she said. 'Good old Yukio! I should have known he'd use the best equipment!'

'Everything seems to be as you say. We don't have sound, unfortunately. That uses extra battery and has to be deliberately turned on remotely – when on battery these cameras only record visuals. There's a lot of footage of you lot standing around and talking to each other.'

He looked at her for a long moment. Then shifted in his seat and let the pause drag a little longer, as though having two conflicting thoughts.

'And?' Manny asked.

He pursed his lips and looked down.

'This is the mightiest mess I've ever come across in my long years. And I'll never know or be able to prove exactly what you all said to each other. But from what I've seen, there's no reason for me to doubt your version of events.'

'Right,' said Manny. She had not been aware that her testimony was in danger of being questioned. It was a new thought. She thought about this new thought. Then nodded. 'Right!' she said again. She held up her hand for a high five, which the inspector looked at, until it was slowly withdrawn.

'On balance,' he said, 'I think going through something as traumatic as this sequence of deaths, and having your career murdered to boot, is probably punishment enough for whatever mistakes you made. Having no reason to suspect you of any agency in these deaths, I'm prepared to release you.'

Manny was knackered. She'd been knackered in her time but this was another whole level beneath. She nodded along with the words as he spoke. And a full two seconds after he'd finished speaking, the meaning of what he'd said arrived in her brain all shining and puffing like the Hogwarts Express.

'Huh!' she said.

He pushed the folder of papers back over the desk to her.

'You're free to go. But – well, try and be a bit more responsible next time. Will you?'

She held up her hand for another high five.

He looked at it.

'I'm just kidding this time,' she said. And, winking at him, she picked up the folder and sashayed out of the interrogation room.

Police Interview Transcript

Interviewee: Damian Shraw

Age: 54

Inspector Constable: So, once and for all,
you requested that the cameraman place a
camera on the chandelier?

Shraw: [Holds hands up.] Wait a minute. Let's
be quite clear. I requested he put a camera
on that chandelier, yes. But I *demanded* that
he do it with full safety gear and as part
of a team of three.

Inspector: The other two being? Seeing as
you've already told me you were running a
skeleton crew?

Shraw: Well, me, and, as it happens, the cleaning lady. Mrs Greggory. She was a bit of a liability . . .

Inspector: You surprise me. Go on.

Shraw: All she had to do was hold a ladder! But, well, yeah, she was half blind. And kind of bonkers, too. Always put all the board games (which were supposed to be in the games room) underneath the Dodecahedral Table, where no one could find them.

Inspector: So after filming ten episodes of the series, you wanted a new camera angle?

Shraw: No, that's the last thing I wanted. We really needed to get footage of those rodents. If they were in the toilets outside that was bad enough. But if they were getting into the entrance hall we were due for any damage they did, and our insurance would triple.

Inspector: Insurance again. It seems to be a motivating factor . . .

Shraw: Have you not noticed that almost all modern human activity is dominated by insurance?

Inspector: Is it? I mean, no, I haven't.

Shraw: If I told you that the beginning
of the First World War and the death of
Trotsky were both caused by failed insurance
policies, would you believe me?

Inspector: I don't know. I suppose so.
Were they?

Shraw: No, they weren't. They were both
famously caused by other things. But the
fact you were willing to consider the idea
for a second shows I'm right. Insurance is
an insidious nightmare!

Chapter Thirty-seven

S tanding outside the Scottish police station, Manny felt the refreshing breeze and looked up into the scraped-clean, calm blue sky that so often follows a large storm.

She turned on the phone that had just been returned to her by the police. Felt it reassuringly erupt into buzzing as messages came through.

She wanted to get home. Get into bed. Be with her first love ... television. Maybe watch *Columbo* again. *After all,* she thought, *there is one thing I don't quite understand ...*

This one thing had several parts. She considered them one by one.

She walked away from the station, keeping an eye out for a cab but mainly looking at her phone.

Firstly, she thought, *did you not notice or did you not mention that, during that whole night, I was never once facing a camera when I was speaking? Did neither you, Constable Sergeant or whatever your name is, nor your Constable Handjob or whatever his name is, notice that while analysing the footage?*

There were sixteen answerphone messages. Seventeen. No, nineteen. That felt better. No! Twenty-one.

Secondly, 'career murdered'? You police don't understand how showbiz works, that's obvious.

Seeing as it was front-page news all around the world, *The Faithfuls* had already, naturally, been renewed for at least another three series. *Not* seasons. 'And we're in a very good position to negotiate your return,' said her agent in a message. 'Because I've already got two six-figure offers for other Saturday night shows. One called *Boss Battle*, which I think sounds good, and another called *Librarian Death Match* which sounds stupid but I love it. Call me back.'

But more importantly, and thirdly, is there anything that happened in this concatenation of catastrophes – this seven-hour silent horror movie you sat through, a hundred years after silent movies went out of date, that proves what I said? People acted in the ways that I told you, but could they not have been manipulated? Or is it all too preposterous?

The next message, presumably left soon after the first, was also from her agent.

'Yeah, well, I should have guessed: there's a seven-figure offer for movie rights, for your version of what happened. I'll see if I can push that into being an eight-figure offer. It's pressing my luck but I don't think it's *impossible* . . . Anyway, who to play you? Sandra Bullock?'

'Sandra Bollocks,' said Manny. 'Angelina Jolie more like, darling.'

Let's imagine that someone did know about the poison that killed Judith. While we're imagining things, let's say Yukio had seen it and in his innocence told this someone where it was, to make sure she didn't touch it. And in the panic, she'd slipped out and made a cup of tea for Judith without anyone noticing. Perhaps she had already teased Yukio not to be such a wet fish about safety

*procedure, and to mount the camera on the chandelier himself –
after greasing the banister he needed to hold onto, to do so.*

*If our imagination extends this far, maybe we could let it take
us further still . . .*

*Maybe this same person was aware of the car, and had indeed
cut its brakes. (And how would a professional middle-aged woman
know to do such things?* YouTube, *darling!) Perhaps this person
also knew full well that the storm was coming, and loosened the
fastenings on that hideously dangerous pike, so that it would fall
and impale anyone who tried to get it down off the wall.*

*Such a person, making all these plans, would no doubt have
found the chance phone signal that took the group out to the car
fortuitous – but even without the signal she could easily have manipulated them into finding it anyway. This mysterious theoretical
person.*

If she exists.

*And finally, Constable Inspector, let's consider the idea that
someone could have wound up all the remaining miserable suspects
to such a pitch of paranoia that they killed each other? Again –
fortuitous that they did so so efficiently. Any last survivors would
have had to have been lured outside to die mysteriously from ex-
posure. But it proved unnecessary. All of them so gullible, all of
them so . . .*

. . . Faithful.

A taxi stopped at her wave, and she got in.

*Only one person, after all, could have done all those things.
And why would they want to? Why 'murder' their own career,
as you say? It seems so implausible. Impossible.*

Unless, of course, they're not who you think they are.

As she stepped off the kerb, she dropped the folder of
papers into a nearby bin.

No use now.

And while the car sped towards the train station, she wriggled comfortably into the leather upholstery. God, so comfortable.

So long, inspector, and good luck. I just wish I knew ... whether you have any suspicions?

Chapter Thirty-eight

I n the station, Inspector Constable was settling down to the soul-wearying task of the mountain of paperwork that faced him. It would take weeks.

There was something that didn't sit right with him, though. (Perhaps Mrs Constable's enthusiastic consumption of *Columbo* was making its influence felt here. She and Manny had plenty in common after all.)

He stood up and examined his damned uncomfortable chair. Right enough, there was a peanut in one of the creases. He dropped it into the bin and sat down again.

Still, something wasn't quite right . . .

He looked at the phone on his desk. Picked up the handset, put it down. Hesitated.

Picked it up again, and dialled.

When it connected, he delivered all his grave doubts down the line in a swift, intense speech. He waited for a beat.

'What do you think, detective chief superintendent?' he asked.

'WHAT THE CHRIST DO YOU MEAN PHONING

ME WITH THIS DRIVEL?' yelled the voice at the other end of the line. The phone jumped in Constable's fingers, slithered like an eel and he had to catch it with both hands.

'Er ... DCS Leaming?'

'WHO THE DEVIL DID YOU EXPECT IT TO BE? YOU'RE EVEN STUPIDER THAN I REMEMBER, CONSTABLE! I'VE SWALLOWED SNOTS THAT HAVE MORE INTELLIGENCE AND INGENUITY THAN YOU COULD SHOW IN A MONTH OF SUNDAYS! YOUR MOTHER WAS RIGHT ABOUT YOU ...'

'My *mother*?' asked Constable, bewildered.

'WHATEVER SHE SAID – AND I'M SURE IT WASN'T KIND – SHE WAS CORRECT TO A GODDAMN T. NOT THAT SHE CAN HAVE BEEN MUCH OF A WOMAN TO CREATE SUCH A ...'

It is not at all necessary (or edifying) to share the rest of the conversation with the reader verbatim. It might instead be best for all parties if a condensed 'safe for work' version was substituted.

Inspector Constable expressed surprise that DCS Totterill had lasted so little time in the job.

DCS Leaming replied that it was not in the least surprising given that she was such a useless stream of epithets.

Inspector Constable replied he was gratified that the old chief was back in the chair, and hoped he wasn't missing the golf course.

DCS Leaming requested that Constable keep his insincere congratulations to himself and asserted he still had two keen eyes on the junior officer. Besides which, you can get thrown out of golf-club bars these days for just opening your mouth and golfers were a big pile of jessies that wanted locking up. Scottish national sport or no.

Inspector Constable suavely moved the conversation on to his suspicions of the celebrity Manny Claudwinkle and his reasons for them.

DCS Leaming informed the inspector what he could do with his suspicions, as Mrs Leaming was fond of 'ye wee spindly lass' on *I Insist You Accompany Me Dancing* on Sunday nights, and if he thought she was a murderer then Constable needed his head examined, which he probably did anyway, but not on the bloody constabulary purse, he could do it in his own time. And the sooner the better. And not to darken the chief superintendent's door etc., etc.

There was a thunderous silence after Inspector Constable put his phone down. The bruising quiet that follows a cacophony.

For a while he walked around the office like someone whose head had happened to find itself between two crashing cymbals, before settling down to work again. He was tempted to take up the train of thought he'd had before, but what the DCS said, the DCS meant. This department – it was like a police state.

So, to paperwork then.

It was standard procedure, especially when investigating multiple murders with an unknown assailant (which he was now gradually and reluctantly starting to accept that this might *not* in fact be), to read over urgent incident reports, which list all other suspicious deaths and violent crimes in the UK (of which there is not a gigantic number in any usual twenty-four-hour period). A daily bulletin was sent to all police stations in the country. And there it was, three pages long, hanging on the bulletin board just outside Constable's office.

He was too tired and dejected to consider doing this.

He didn't want to read about hold-ups in Hastings, armed robberies in Armagh or car-jackings in Conwy when he had this Himalaya of bureaucracy to climb. Instead he strapped on his metaphorical crampons and got to work, humming a nameless tune which was stuck in his head and which someone told him two days' continuous humming later was the theme tune to *The Faithfuls*.

If he had, he would have come across the report of a woman's body found in a sixteenth-floor London flat in an advanced state of decomposition. Thought to be in her fifties. Cause of death, suicide by hanging. Date of death uncertain but probably twelve weeks ago. Just before filming commenced on the new series of *The Faithfuls*, he may have inwardly noted. Name of victim thought to be Smith, Jill. No known relatives.

But if he had read it, it's doubtful he would have made a connection.

Chapter Thirty-nine

C ecil walked towards Hannah, wielding the mighty axe. 'It was me and Fiona all along,' Hannah said, turning her gun on him. 'We've been having an affair behind your back. Now our plan has come to fruition. Time to die!'

'Not so fast, you murdering bitch!' said Manny, cartwheeling towards her, wielding a samurai sword. 'This is the part where *you* die!'

With a graceful swish of the blade, Manny performed a dextrous leap and came to earth with the poise of a ballet dancer, sword arm pointed forward. She looked along the glinting blade and a tell-tale bean of blood running towards her told her she'd found her mark.

Behind her, Hannah's severed head smacked to the floor surrounded by a pattering cascade of gore.

'And ... *cut*,' said a voice. 'That was good. One more time though. Let's go again.'

Manny handed the sword to a prop assistant, who wiped it assiduously. She saw someone in the corner behind the lights and went over. It was another Manny.

'Honey,' said the actress, 'so good to see you.'

'Angelina, darling,' said the other. 'You're killing it. Literally! I love it. I love *you*.'

They walked between banks of technicians preparing the next take. One with nothing to do leant against a ladder reading the inner pages of a tabloid, whose front page announced: CLAUDWINKLE AND HUSBAND SPLIT. Just visible beneath the fold of the page was the subheading: 'Not the Woman I Married, says Spouse of Murder Spree Survivor Star'.

'Was it really like this?' Angelina asked, gesturing to the blood-spattered set of the Mead Hall.

'Course it was. Exactly. You've got it to a T. Now off you go and chop her head off again, you busy vigilante. I don't want to keep you. Just wanted to pop my head in and see you in action.'

'Watch the next take. It'll be better,' said Angelina, returning to her mark, as she was handed a clean katana.

'Lights are set. Are we on our marks?' the director, McG, said. Manny had particularly requested him. His brand of wild entertainment was to her taste. 'We don't want a documentary, do we, darling?' she'd said at the pitch meeting. 'I mean, let's get some bums on seats here, am I right?'

'Ms Claudwinkle,' an assistant whispered in her ear. 'Your car is here.'

'One more minute,' said Manuela. She wasn't watching what was happening on the set. She was thinking of another scene and reliving it.

It was in the living room of a council flat in a London housing estate.

Faith Meadows was staring wonderingly into the eyes of Jill Smith.

'Do you *really* think I could take the part on?'

Jill shrugged. 'Only one way to find out. It's the most bloody fun I ever had. Give it a go, what have you got to lose?'

Faith nodded. There was wisdom in this.

'Just don't fuck it up,' said Jill. 'And of course, if you *do* get famous and make millions, bear in mind I might hunt you down and kill you. And take her back,' she added. 'If it so happens my life isn't going so well. I'm a cold, calculating bitch, after all.'

Faith laughed. Jill didn't.

Faith didn't notice. She was staring at the wig.

Remembering the scene, her brain whirring, Manny fingered the mole in the corner of her eye, without knowing that she did so. (It was her new mannerism that her extra legion of super-fans explained as a nervous tic bequeathed by the horrors she'd endured – and there was some truth in that, as well. But they didn't know she'd been doing it for thirty years.)

There was something bothering her. One last thing . . .

She watched Angelina slice the bonce off the other woman in a spray of blood. *Gah, that never gets old*, she thought. *Just like me. What* was *I trying to remember?*

Oh yes.

Taking her phone out, she went to her emails and permanently deleted a message from Jill Smith, inviting Manny to come over for tea if she had a chance, before the seventh series of *The Faithfuls* started. To catch up on old times. If the police ever looked at Jill's own computer (which they had precious little reason to), they would find the message deleted from her email account as well.

She'd made sure of that.

'And ... ACTION!' yelled the director.